Uncarved
A Nornir Saga

By: Kira Shay

FSF Publications

Cover art and design by Covers by Christian

Print ISBN 978-1-950532-06-3
e-book ISBN 978-1-950532-07-0

Manufactured in the United States of America.

www.fivesmilingfish.com

<u>**Also by Five Smiling Fish:**</u>

Kira Shay:
Angel's Prophecy
Legend of the Strega
Azra's Guide to (Bad) Parenting
Fair to Middling

Megan Vaughn:
The Emerald Door
Fable of the Immortals

Anthologies:
From the Darkest Corner

Check out the above titles at:
www.fivesmilingfish.com

Dedicated to: Rachel Woodruff
Who wanted to know what happened after the first page and was patient enough to wait two years for the rest of the story.

Endless thanks and appreciation to:

Will, for humoring the voices in my head and loving me despite the trouble they get me into.

Sidney Reetz and Megan Vaughn for listening to me prattle on about all the research I did. And for encouraging me to do more along the way.

Beth Lake for the edits.

Amanda Griffis and Matt Bergren for your honest opinions and your cheerleading.

Tom Dushku for the technical assistance.

Dr. Jackson Crawford for his notions on knowledge sharing and incredible YouTube library of information.

And thanks to YOU for reading!

Old Norse	English	Meaning
Æsir	Aesir	Tribe of Gods
Álfheimr	Alfheim	Realm of the Elves
Angantýr	Angantyr	Norse Folk Hero
Argr	Argr	Old Norse insult- unmanly
Ásgarðr	Asgard	Realm of the Aesir
Bifrǫst	Bifrost	Rainbow bridge between Asgard and Midgard
Brynhildr	Brunhilde	Valkyrie/ Folk Heroine
Drengr	Drengr	Old Norse honor- manliness
Freyja	Freya	Vanir Goddess of Beauty
Heimdallr	Heimdal	Watcher/ Guardian of the Bifrost
Himinbjǫrg	Himminbjorg	Heimdall's hall in Asgard
Iðunn	Idunn	Goddess of Immortality
Ífingr	Ifingr	River separating Asgard and Jotunheim
Jǫrmungandr	Jormungander	World Serpent
Jǫtnar	Jotnar	Plural of Giant
Jǫtunheimr	Jotunheim	Realm of the Giants
Jǫtunn	Jotun	Giant
Miðgarðr	Midgard	Realm of the Humans (Earth)
Mímir	Mimir	Guardian of the Well of Wisdom
Múspellsheimr	Muspelheim	Realm of Fire
Niðavellir	Nidavallir	Realm of the Dwarves
Niðhǫggr	Nidhog	Serpent who gnaws on the roots of Yggdrasil
Nifilheimr	Nifilheim	Realm of Fog
Njǫrðr	Njord	God of the Sea
Óðinn	Odin	Chief God of the Aesir
Ragnarǫk	Ragnarok	end of the world
Ratatǫskr	Ratatosk	Squirrel who lives in Yggdrasil
Samsø	Samso	Island in Midgard
Seiðr	Seidr	a type of witchcraft

Old Norse	English	Meaning
Skírnir	Skirnir	Freyr's Servant
Þórr	Thor	God of Thunder
Týrfingr	Tyrfing	Name of a mythological sword
Urðr	Urd	Norn of the Past
Valhǫll	Valhalla	Odin's hall in Asgard
Veðrfǫlnir	Verdfolnir	Eagle at the top of Yggdrasil
Verðandi	Verdandi	Norn of the Present
Vǫlva	Volva	Seer/ witch

Chapter One: The Tree

Runes don't lie. This had to be a mistake.

Skuld closed her ice-like eyes and poised her obsidian dagger against the trunk of the World Tree, Yggdrasil. Taking in a deep, steadying breath, her hand moved once more. The edge of the blade scratched into the thick bark creating a string of jointed figures. When she opened her eyes, the nine glowing and freshly etched runes were the same as the ones she'd carved before.

Runes don't lie, but could they be wrong?

The young Norn brushed her dark hair out of her face and sheathed her dagger as she contemplated the carving before her. The runes were not what they should be despite her attempt to change them. That meant the events foretold in those carvings were irreversible, creating a new fixed point in the current cycle of Yggdrasil. Or rather, if what she read could be believed, the end of Yggdrasil and all who dwelled in its branches.

She began her descent from the lowest branch of the great tree. Her sisters needed to know what the runes predicted. Perhaps they would have more insight into such a disturbing message.

Above her the cosmos stretched into eternity, the inky blackness punctuated by plumed clouds of light from nearby galaxies. Yggdrasil stood tall and resolute against the backdrop of the universe. Its branches extended far and wide, supporting nine realms of existence amongst its leaves.

"Sisters, something strange will happen," Skuld called as she dropped onto the patch of terrain that supported the well. Eager to get their attention, she sprinted the short distance past the hut which served as their home to the Well of Destiny.

One of the three water sources that fed the roots of Yggdrasil, the well itself was small; a babbling spring with iridescent water that collected in an oblong-shaped pool that never got deeper than Skuld's waist. The water shimmered over white mud. Nothing swam in its transparent depths, though Skuld had spent hours watching the undercurrents swirling the mud into different patterns.

Verðandi, the Norn of the Present, glanced at her younger sister briefly, her attention focused on gathering handfuls of white mud in a wide clay bowl. She perched at the edge of the pool, her feet submerged in the water. "We are busy right now. Can it wait?"

"No, it is urgent," Skuld stated and planted her hands on her narrow hips. It was always difficult to get Verðandi to stop what she was doing.

Having filled the bowl, Verðandi stood and moved out of the water and towards the other side of the trunk where a fresh coating of the nutrient-filled mud was needed. She flipped her long, light brown braid out of her way before dipping her mud-caked hands into the bowl and slathering the contents onto the exposed bark. The runes on her fingernails glowed through the thick mud.

"You know better than to interrupt her when she is focused on a task. Have you not yet learned it is unwise to disrupt the Keeper of the Present from her work?" Urðr commented as she emerged from the hut. She clutched a tall wooden staff carved from a fallen limb of the World Tree. She leaned against it as she walked with her robe dragging along the ground in her wake. While Urðr was the oldest of the Nornir, it would be a mistake to think her frail and weak. Her slate-gray eyes rimmed with faint echoes of the past saw through to the very core of a person. "You're troubled, Sister. What have you seen?"

"The runes . . . they foretell the end of all."

Urðr tsked dismissively. "With each season of death, a season of rebirth soon follows. Creation and destruction dance together, always closely bound. What once was will be again. The cycle of Yggdrasil and all of the Nine Realms has been carved many times over. The runes are always cast this way."

Skuld shook her head, trying to find the right words to explain what she'd seen. "It is true; we three have guided and shaped the Nine Realms through countless springs of creation and winters of destruction. But the runes fell different this time. There won't be another rebirth. Yggdrasil itself will die. We will die."

Urðr frowned at her youngest sister, her eyes narrowing. "Yggdrasil will not die. It will sleep for a time, but it always comes back. This is how it has always been and how it always will be. The cycle never changes. The runes are simply warning of Ragnarǫk."

"The destruction of Ragnarǫk is not upon us," Verðandi called, wiping her face with her forearm. She left a smear of the white silt along her cheekbone. With the empty bowl dangling from her hand, she returned to the edge of the well. "The Æsir gods and the Vanir gods are preparing to wage their war presently."

"She is right," Skuld said. "The events necessary for the death cycle of Ragnarǫk have not yet come to pass. I have yet to carve them into the tree. Sisters, the runes I just drew say those events will never happen. Instead, they foretold Veðrfǫlnir, the eagle atop of Yggdrasil will abandon his nest. The serpent Niðhǫggr who gnaws on the roots of the great tree will fall ill. The well he guards will be left unattended. Mímir, the guardian of the Well of Knowledge will die protecting his charge. The Well of

Destiny we guard will be contaminated and poison the very core of the World Tree. The great Yggdrasil and all within would wither and rot. All who live among the branches of the tree will die. Its lifeless remains will float endlessly into the universe. The steady pace of fate and the power we command will falter until it ceases completely. Sisters, we face extinction." Speaking the words out loud made the truth of them sink into Skuld's heart. She didn't want to believe, but the runes were never wrong.

"You have made a mistake," Urðr said at last, though doubt shaded her words. "Have you tried to coerce the runes to a different route?"

"Yes, and they came out the same. It seems we do not have the power to change this destiny."

The three Nornir lapsed into pensive silence. The thought of their demise never before crossed their minds. They were eternal and powerful, much like Yggdrasil itself. Their function was simple; keep the great cosmic ash tree healthy and nourished and to ensure the cycles of destruction and creation were followed in the appropriate manner for all the realms. They achieved these things by guarding the Well of Destiny to make sure its waters remained pure and fresh. They coated the exposed roots and bark with the white silt from the spring to better nourish the tree. And they carved the runes that guided the fate of all the realms which existed within Yggdrasil's branches. When all the realms experienced destruction at Ragnarǫk, the fate runes vanished, their purpose having been fulfilled. The sisters, however, always remained to continue their work, to continue to care for Yggdrasil. Except now the runes foretold they would not.

Verðandi spoke first, sorrow tinging her words, "If Skuld cannot change the runes then we cannot stop this destiny. Until the end comes, we must hold fast to our duties. We must accept this fate."

"I will not accept it!" Skuld swore. "Urðr, you must know, has Yggdrasil itself ever been threatened before?" A shred of hope shone in her voice, clothed in desperation.

Urðr thought about the question, her gaze growing distant as her focus slipped backward through all the regenerations of Yggdrasil. After a time, she sighed and told her sisters, "No, the cycle has always been the same. This is the first time the runes have foretold our death. Sister, did you see any milestones to this horrific fate? Any fixed points of importance?"

Skuld pursed her lips, thinking of the strange etching. Her sight into the future became hazy. The images which usually came with ease were now broken and shifted, almost as though the future changed too fast for her to grasp it. Worry gnawed at the edges of her thoughts. Was she losing her powers? She tamped down the thought before she could be distracted by the doubt.

She spoke in short, halting sentences attempting to convey the shifting and blurred images. "Ragnarǫk does not occur as it must, though the cause is hidden from my view. I cannot tell who or what is directing this chaos."

Verðandi wrung her hands together, fretting as she was wont to do when important things were just beyond the here and now. "Did something happen to put us on this course?" Verðandi asked, looking at Urðr. "Have we missed something in the past that changed our fate?"

"I see nothing," the old Norn admitted. Concern deepened the wrinkles on her brow.

"If Urðr cannot see what has happened to cause this," Verðandi rambled on, her panic seeking some sort of outlet, "then there are too many paths which lead to this end. I cannot see anything in the present out of the ordinary. There is no one definitive thing that can untangle the web of cause and effect. There is nothing we can do. The runes are set."

"How soon?" Urðr asked, holding up her hand to

silence Verðandi's rising alarm.

The two sisters waited in tense anticipation as Skuld formed her answer.

"By the way the runes fell, it will start within the span of three dusks in the Nine Realms. I cannot tell what the first event will be. That was not shown."

"What should we do?" Verðandi asked. Silence met her question as they all thought and exchanged worried glances.

At last, Urðr spoke up. "We should alert the others who live in relation to Yggdrasil. They have a right to know what is coming. We will see if the runes Skuld carved have truth in them. I will meet with the serpent Niðhǫggr, Guardian of the First Well among the deepest roots. Perhaps the primordial waters will tell a different story than the runes."

Verðandi piped up, "I will visit the deer among the mid-branches. Maybe they have seen strange comings and goings between the realms where they graze."

"I will travel with Verðandi to the mid-branches and then I will continue to the top of the tree to seek out Veðrfǫlnir," Skuld said, adding, "And I'll tell the squirrel Ratatǫskr, if I can find him."

With their destinations mapped out, the three sisters embraced in farewell, each harboring trepidation at what they might find.

"The journeys will take days. Return as quickly as possible to compare what we've discovered. Safe travels, my sisters," Urðr bid them as she shuffled her way to the twisting roots, leaning on her staff. If she followed the right root, it would eventually take her to the home of the great serpent Niðhǫggr who guarded Hvergelmir, the oldest of the three wells.

Verðandi went into the hut made of fallen branches and thick leaves. When she emerged, she held both Skuld's travel cloak and her own. She donned the cloak. As she fastened it at her throat with a crafted broach pin, she told her younger sister, "We must hurry. The mid-branches are at least two days journey from here."

Skuld took her own dark woven cloak. She gave a sharp whistle aimed at the dense foliage above her home and waited.

A rustling of leaves accompanied the whoosh of beating wings. With a screech, a large white and brown colored owl emerged from the leaves, his speckled wings wide and arching. He dove straight for Skuld, headfirst. The Norn raised her left arm and, in a sudden upswing, the owl's talons flashed before the creature landed gingerly upon her.

Skuld clicked her tongue at the bird. He responded by clicking in kind as he sidestepped up her arm and settled on her shoulder. "We are going to visit Veðrfǫlnir, Strix," Skuld explained as she ran her fingers over the owl's head.

Strix hooted and folded his wings close to his body, content to ride on her shoulder for the time being.

Together, Skuld and Verðandi set off around the trunk of the tree, finding their way to the path that would take them to mid-branches where the four deer liked to nibble the tender shoots from the bark of Yggdrasil.

The undergrowth which thrived among the roots of the great tree receded around a dirt path that led from the Nornir home to the dwelling of the deer. Roots arched overhead before plunging back into the ground on the other side. Ferns and wildflowers grew with wild abandon. Some reached as tall as Skuld's waist. The air was damp and filled with the aroma of decay and growth. High above the thick roots of the tree, giant leaves fluttered against the backdrop of the endless universe.

"What can we do to prepare for the future the runes gave you?" Verðandi asked. She watched her sister from the corner of her eye. "This journey to talk to all of the inhabitants of the tree is noble and right, but there must be something more we can do."

Skuld shook her head. "I do not know. The runes didn't give any more clues; just what I've already told you and Urðr."

Verðandi fiddled with the edges of her cloak, a frown creating worry lines around her mouth.

A stab of concern lanced through Skuld. Her sister was not one to worry and fret. Verðandi had always been rooted in the present. This shift, this change in her sister fueled the fear her rune carving had instilled inside of herself.

"We start climbing here," Verðandi halted her gait and motioned to a root that doubled back over to the trunk.

Skuld waited for her sister to go first. Strix flapped his wings and removed himself from Skuld's shoulder, allowing her to climb freely. He kept pace with their climb, flying a short distance and waiting for the sisters to catch up before continuing upwards.

Because of the urgency of their mission, the two sisters climbed as quickly as they could. They passed most of their usual rest spots in their haste. By the time they reached the halfway point of their journey, Skuld's muscles ached and exhaustion threatened to make her lose her grip.

"We must rest," Verðandi stated as Skuld reached the small plateau. An overhang of bark provided a suitable place to stop.

Skuld nodded as she brushed the dirt from her hands on her trousers. "Yes, we do need to rest. When you are ready to continue, keep the pace we have been traveling; I think you can reach the mid-branches a day early."

Verðandi didn't miss the distinction. "You are not coming with me to see the deer?"

"No, I will travel on using the opposite path. It is more difficult, but it is also quicker in the long run."

Together, the sisters settled down to rest. While the

roots were far below, the thick foliage of the mid-branches were just as far above. From their vantage point of peering upwards, the shimmer that indicated the presence of one of the realms could be seen refracting the light from the nearest stars. Through the distorted watery shimmer, vague landscapes could be seen.

"It is Alfheim," Verðandi said.

Skuld stroked Strix's head and glanced upwards. "It is."

Verðandi continued, her gazed fixed on the realm of the elves. "It is dusk there. The end of the first day. Your runes said the catastrophe would come within three dusks in the realms did they not?"

Skuld shifted uneasily. Sensing his mistress's distress, Strix nuzzled his cheek against her fingertips, letting out a soft hoot of reassurance. "That is what it felt like. Three dusks within the realms and then the end will begin."

"But they did not say for sure how long we have?"

"No. They did not say for sure."

The two lapsed into pensive silence. Keeping her thoughts to herself, Verðandi shifted so that her back was to her sister. Eventually, soft snoring came from where she slept.

Skuld remained awake, watching the hazy colors shift from light to dark in the realm swirling above her.

"I don't know what to do, Strix," Skuld murmured, glancing over at her winged friend. "I don't know what will happen and it scares me."

Strix hooted back at her, fluffing his wings and shifting his head. He blinked his large ponderous eyes as though trying to reassure her.

Skuld sighed and stroked his feathers once again. "Thank you, my friend."

With troubled thoughts and a nameless sense of dread, Skuld closed her eyes and fell into a fitful sleep.

A little while later, Skuld opened her eyes to find

Verðandi standing over her.

"It is time to go. We dare not waste any more time." Having made this pronouncement, Verðandi flipped her brown braid to her back and fastened her cloak.

Skuld got to her feet, her muscles still aching from the fast-paced climb the day before. She shook her cloak out and fastened it around her neck.

Verðandi took her hand and squeezed it meaningfully. "Take care. The climb to the top is perilous. Do not lose your footing."

"I won't," Skuld promised. "See you back home soon, sister." She watched Verðandi climb towards the mid-branches where the deer resided.

When Verðandi was out of sight, Skuld started her journey up the tree to the top-most branches where a giant eagle perched and watched the ever-swirling cosmos.

At first, the climb was easy enough; the small branches on the lower portion of the trunk were often traversed by the three sisters in their duties. However, the higher she climbed the less familiar the path became. The branches stretched farther apart with only the pale expanse of the thick trunk connecting them. It took her the better portion of the day to approach the middle section of the great ash. She rested only briefly before continuing. This portion of the journey required her to free climb the trunk itself.

Strix took flight as his mistress began climbing in earnest, perching at the next highest branch until she caught up. Skuld's hands and feet found small crevices along the trunk to keep her moving ever upward for what seemed like an eternity. Soon, her muscles began to tremble and ache with the exertion of the ascent. Along the way she rested as long as she dared, the ominous runes always in the back of her mind, nudging her ever upward.

Eventually, more branches were clustered close

enough together that she could walk along the limbs and hoist herself up to the next one. The higher she got, the narrower the trunk and subsequent branches became until they were too small to hold her weight.

At last, she couldn't get any higher.

"Strix," she called as she clung precariously to a thin, wobbling branch. "Where is Veðrfǫlnir?"

The owl hooted twice from his nearby perch as if to say he didn't know.

Skuld squinted against the brightness of the nearby galaxies, searching for any hint of the giant eagle. Then she spotted a large bundle of twigs and leaves interspersed with feathers of incredible size no more than a few feet away from her. She found the nest!

Skuld sidled her way over to the edge of the nest that towered well above her head. Without hesitation, she climbed to the top and peered in only to see nothing but a thick layer of down feathers coating an under layer of brittle twigs and sticks.

A thrill of fear coursed through her blood as she scanned the rest of the branches. There was nothing in the upper reaches of Yggdrasil except herself and Strix. Veðrfǫlnir could not be found. The warnings of the runes rang in her mind.

A sudden burst of galactic wind buffeted against her back, sending her sprawling face-first into the nest. The stars cartwheeled above her even as the sharp ends of sticks and leaves scratched her through the softness of the down. She landed in a heap at the bottom, covered in feathers and twigs.

Before she could catch her breath, a loud snap and an abrupt lurch underneath her sent her heart pounding into her throat. She grasped desperately to the closest twigs beneath her. One wrong move could cause the bottom to break apart.

Skuld stretched out her arm towards the edge of the nest. She had to get back down the tree and tell her sisters that Veðrfǫlnir disappeared, just as the runes foretold.

The shift of her weight caused the material beneath her to snap and crack. The hand supporting her weight punched through the bottom of the nest and soon the rest of her followed suit as she fell.

There was no time to scream. Frantic, she grasped for anything to hold onto as she plummeted from the top of the World Tree. She succeeded in grabbing onto one of the leaves from the swiftly passing limbs. The leaf ripped away from the branch and Skuld continued her rapid descent.

Despite the terrible fear pounding through her veins, she had the presence of mind to maneuver the giant leaf beneath her. While it did slow her down, her weight was too much to allow a gentle flutter to the bottom of the tree. Gripping either side of it tightly, she attempted to steer her newfound vehicle around the obstacles of other branches and flying bark.

The landscape of the tree passed by in a blur of color. The faint color shifts which marked the different realms in the branches smeared together into a kaleidoscope that made Skuld ill to her stomach. After falling for ages, she made a hard landing at the base of the great tree. She lost her grip on the edges of the leaf and dove towards the terrain, tumbling heavily amongst the hardwood. When she came to a halt, it knocked the very air out of her lungs and her vision went dark.

Skuld heard Strix hooting above her before she became fully aware of the ache racing through her body. With her head booming, she slowly blinked her eyes open. Strix was indeed above her, perched on one of the exposed roots nearby. He hooted and blinked at her as she slowly remembered her rough landing.

"How long was I unconscious?" she asked the bird.

He flapped his wings a couple of times before settling them back against his body.

Skuld craned her neck so she could look up at the sky, though it made her head pound more. The galactic bodies that she and her sisters used to mark the passage of time were much farther along their paths than when she had last seen them at the top of the tree. She had lost a significant amount of time; more than she would have liked. She had to get back to the well.

Skuld scowled as she untwisted her limbs and painfully got to her feet. Brushing off her clothes and adjusting her cloak back to its proper place, she set off for her home. As she traversed the arching roots and soft terrain, her mind worried at what she'd seen at the top of the tree. Or rather, what she hadn't seen. She hoped her sisters had also returned so they could decide what to do.

She took the shortest route back to the Well of Destiny, her instincts forcing her to hurry along the path. If Veðrfǫlnir had left, then perhaps some of the other aspects of what she foresaw came to pass too. Her thoughts flitted to the portion of the runes depicting the three wells drying up and their guardians dead.

The long journey coupled with her uncertain hours of unconsciousness made her worry. Was she too late? Skuld found herself running full tilt towards the well. Dread weighed each step. Strix flew above her, sensing her urgency.

At last, she saw the edges of the hut just around the bend. With a sudden burst of energy, she accelerated her pace even more until the well came into sight.

What she saw brought her up short. A strangled gasp escaped her throat as shock, anguish, and rage washed over her all at once.

A horrible stench of death and decay permeated the air. The usually crystal-clear waters of the spring were a deep, muddy crimson. The nourishing white silt had been stained a dark red. In the middle of a thick puddle of blood and gore laid the decapitated corpse of the squirrel, Ratatǫskr.

Skuld froze in place as she took in the sight of the dead creature who had once been her friend. She noted with horrified shock how blood matted his fur; his red fur had been so soft when he was alive. His sparkling brown eyes were now lifeless and glazed. Had it been the other day they laughed together at the latest trade of insults between Veðrfǫlnir and Niðhǫggr?

"Oh, my friend," she whispered, stunned and sickened at the scene. "You were not supposed to die. Not like this."

Forcing herself to face not only the demise of her friend, but also the horrific manner in which it happened, Skuld stepped closer to the corpse looking for any sort of clue to tell her who was responsible for such a heinous act. Ignoring the stench, she knelt in the gore. After pushing back the bile that found its way into her mouth, she shifted Ratatǫskr's severed head to inspect it.

Wider than her whole body with his tufted ears coming to her shoulders, his head was heavier than she expected and it took both of her hands and a surprising amount of force to move it on its side. Upon examination, the cut that severed his head was not clean; whatever weapon had been employed for the job was used poorly. Several strokes were needed to complete the task. The intentional infliction of suffering on Ratatǫskr made the icy fury in her veins swell. Judging by the color of the congealing blood, the murder happened not long after the sisters had set out on their respective errands.

Strix hooted, low at his mistress.

"I know," she answered, still fixating on her inspection of the body.

Ratatǫskr's mouth twisted in a painful grimace, exposing his sharp teeth. Something fluttered from the corner of his mouth, drawing Skuld's attention. Leaning closer, she pried out what appeared to be a shred of green fabric from between his back teeth. Through the bloodstains, Skuld saw a fine silk weave with intricate silver specks embedded into a pattern commonly found in Álfheimr, one of the nine worlds in the branches of Yggdrasil. The quality of the silk and the delicate craftsmanship identified the owner of it as nobility.

As she ripped the fabric out of Ratatǫskr's mouth, she asked Strix, "Why would someone from the high elven families do something like this? To what purpose?" She waved the fabric aloft.

Strix shifted his weight from one foot to another.

With Ratatǫskr's blood soaking her boots and the edges of her cape, Skuld scanned the terrain around the well. Whoever killed him must have left some tracks. Sure enough, foreign footprints were embedded in the mud. They were smaller than hers, but uniform in appearance, which meant the murderer wore shoes.

An irresistible need to track down whoever did this and remove their head with a blunt sword overtook Skuld. The need supplanted her fear and grief and gave her a razor-sharp focus. She screamed her fury into the branches of the tree and slammed her hand into the gore-slicked mud. She wouldn't cry. Not yet. Not until she had her vengeance for Ratatǫskr's murder. With dirty hands, she crammed the piece of fabric into her pocket and followed the footsteps. "Come on, Strix. Whoever did this cannot be far." With Strix flying above her, she stalked away from the body of her friend.

Skuld had never been a very good huntress. Tracking things was not her specialty, but whoever left the bloody imprints hadn't been concerned with covering their trail. They didn't follow any of the well-worn paths she and her sisters used. Either they were in too much of a rush to get away that they didn't notice or they hadn't used them on purpose in the attempt not to run into anyone else. Over exposed roots and under giant ferns, Skuld trailed the reddish mud tracks of the murderer. Across expanses of damp dirt and rock piles, she followed them until the smeared blood trails and the footsteps disappeared.

Casting an agitated gaze at her surroundings and hoping to pick up the trail again, she peered quizzically at where the last bloody mud print stopped. A few feet away was a ledge with a modest opening in the rock face surrounded by ferns and grass. In the distance, she heard the clang of hammers striking hot metal. She realized she stood in front of the entrance of Niðavellir, one of the realms Yggdrasil nourished. It wasn't a grand gateway. In fact, if you weren't paying attention, the cave opening was easy to miss.

Skuld let out a soft curse as she wondered what to do next.

Out of the corner of her eye, something glinted through a thin covering of greenery.

She pulled her dagger from its sheath at her hip as she crept towards the bushes.

"I see you there," she called out. No response came.

In a quick, sharp movement, Skuld pushed the greenery aside and brandished her dagger high above her, ready to jam it forcefully into whoever hid there.

She blinked in confusion when all she saw behind the leaves and twigs was a sword leaning up against a rock as though waiting for her. Confused, Skuld inspected it closer. Half her height, the blade had once been a magnificent weapon. Fresh blood coated the blade and smudged along the golden hilt. The metal no longer shone, leaving Skuld to wonder who would care so little for something so fine.

She picked up the sword, realizing it must have been what brought such an untimely end to Ratatǫskr. It was heavy and unbalanced in her hand, though the blade was still sharp. An odd, angled marking of jumbled runes graced the base of the pommel, but the design wasn't one Skuld had ever seen before.

A sudden loud, sustained shriek broke Skuld's concentration. At once a fresh wave of panic washed through her veins. It sounded like her sister, Verðandi. What if the murderer tricked her into following a false trail? What if her sisters were in danger? Without a moment's hesitation, Skuld broke into a run, determined to get back to the well.

When she arrived, her sisters stood a few paces away from Ratatǫskr's corpse, Urðr with a horrified expression on her face and Verðandi clutching both hands to her mouth.

"Are you hurt?" Skuld barked out, her breaths coming in hard, ragged gasps.

"No, but Ratatǫskr? What happened?" Urðr demanded.

"I don't know," Skuld answered, doing her best to ignore the sticky wetness of the blood congealing on her legs. "I found him this way. I tried to track down the one responsible. I found nothing except this sword."

Urðr squinted at the weapon in confusion.

"This shouldn't be happening," Verðandi asserted, her fear making her voice loud and high.

Skuld lost her patience with her sister's hysterics. "Well, it is happening and worse is to come. Veðrfǫlnir has left Yggdrasil."

The sisters glanced at each other, worry and a growing panic etched into their features.

"Niðhǫggr is ill," Urðr said at last. "He no longer gnaws on the roots but lays there in a stupor. The well Hvergelmir has been poisoned. It bubbles black and foams with putrid stenches I've never beheld before."

"Poisoned? Who would do such a thing?" Verðandi cried.

Skuld chewed her bottom lip, the runes she carved earlier flashing in her mind. "What of the deer?"

With her eyes still riveted on the corpse of the squirrel laying in the stained mud and water, Verðandi piped up, "The deer are all fine. They know nothing of what is happening. I told them to be careful. We must clear the well. We cannot leave it this way."

"No, we have to find who did this and stop them from doing any more damage," Skuld argued. "The one responsible for this travesty is still at large. We must stop them."

"How?" Verðandi demanded. She gestured towards Ratatoskr's lifeless body. "Sisters, this was not supposed to happen. Ratatoskr's murder was not in the runes, not even the ones Skuld carved earlier. The course we are on at present has never been written."

The nine runes she carved earlier danced in Skuld's mind. "Then we need to change it," she answered with more confidence than she felt. "The person who did this . . . they are defying their fate, whatever it may be. If they can do such things, then we can as well. After all, we are the ones who cast the runes. We are the ones who carve the lives into Yggdrasil. If we cannot master our own destiny, then we deserve to die."

"Don't say such things!" Verðandi gasped.

Urðr spoke next, crossing her arms in thought. "You said yourself the things transpiring have not been written. If they have not, then we are not changing them. We are paving our own course."

"Then it's settled," Skuld announced. "We find who did this and make them stop this madness. We will make them pay for the harm they have caused."

"But the well," protested Verðandi. "If we don't clean it then Yggdrasil will certainly suffer. If Hvergelmir has been poisoned, then Yggdrasil will need more fresh water and nutrients to combat it. The Well of Destiny should not remain contaminated. And what should we do with poor Ratatoskr?"

"You are right, sister," Urðr conceded. "It seems we will have to divide our forces. Verðandi, you focus on cleaning the well and setting things to rights. I will search for ways to reverse the runes that call for Yggdrasil's demise. Skuld, you must go into the realms and find the one responsible for this tragedy."

Gripping the hilt of the sword in her fist, Skuld vowed, "I will kill the one responsible."

Urðr cautioned, "No, not kill. Bring them here to us. I would look into the eyes of the creature who dared to destroy Yggdrasil."

"But sister—"

"Do not argue. Perhaps the creature can reverse what it has done."

Verðandi spoke up, "Skuld has never traveled to the realms before. She does not know what to expect. The realm dwellers are strange peoples. They have many customs and protocols for interacting with each other. It would take a lifetime to give her such knowledge."

Urðr took Skuld by the arm. "Then we will give her the most important information. First and foremost, the realms are a contradictory place. The customs of one realm differ from another. However, there is a unifying principle in how they interact. That principle is the rule of hospitality. They have many stories where strangers tend to be gods and can bless or curse them depending on how they are treated. The peoples of the realms tend to err on the side of caution in that respect when it comes to strangers. They will open their homes, feed you at their tables, and not ask many questions of you. Since you will be a stranger in their land they must treat you with respect, even if they do not know your true nature."

Verðandi added, "Not all of the creatures in the realms will recognize you for what you are. The ones who might recognize us on sight are the gods; the Æsir and the Vanir. You needn't worry about them though. Those bickering fools know better than to cross a Norn. We are, after all, one of the few beings who can undo all of their powers and all of their influence."

"Like Ullr," Skuld murmured. "He threatened Verðandi the last time she traveled the realms. When she came back, you and she uncarved him from the tree. How many cycles has it been?"

"It doesn't matter," Verðandi replied. "The important thing is the people of the realms fear the gods and the gods fear us. That should ensure you are treated with the proper respect among all."

Urðr said, "If any in the Nine Realms fails in their duty to be a good host, then it is a grave insult. If you do not retaliate appropriately, then you will be considered weak and many will prey upon you. Give no mercy to insults. The most dangerous thing to be when walking the realms is weak."

Skuld listened to her sisters with wide eyes. "Is that really how the realms are?"

Urðr nodded in affirmation. "You cannot show weakness. Along your journey, see to it as many of the events leading up to Ragnarǫk remain unchanged. Perhaps if the culprit is caught, we can uncarve this destiny and set things back into the proper cycle."

"Where will you begin?" Verðandi asked, tears streaming down her face as she closed Ratatǫskr's eyes.

Skuld tried not to look at the blood coating her sister's hands. The initial fury and shock of Ratatǫskr's death wore off and, in its place, bloomed a pervasive weight in the center of her chest.

"The culprit's footprints led to the entrance of Niðavellir. I will consult with the dwarves. They will know whose weapon this is. I believe it is one of their creations. But I must go and now. There is no time to waste while the murderer is loose."

Urðr and Verðandi moved to embrace their sister and to wish her luck. The three of them held onto each other for a long moment. Tears fell between them, a symbol of their shared grief and the recognition of the new sensation called fear.

"Safe travels, sister," Urðr said.

"Yes, return to us," Verðandi agreed.

"I will," Skuld promised. "And I will bring back the

person responsible."

Skuld and Strix followed the murderer's trail once more to the cave leading into the realm of the dwarves. Strix sailed ahead of her, keeping close enough to warn of trouble.

When they arrived at the entrance to Niðavellir, a wave of uncertainty overtook Skuld. She realized just how blind she was; she didn't know for sure the dwarves would help her. She didn't know anything about the murderer except they wore shoes and didn't know how to wield a sword. She wasn't even sure she was on the right path.

Strix landed on her shoulder and nuzzled her cheek with the top of his head.

"What if this isn't right? Without my sight, how can I tell what should be?"

Strix cooed and rustled his wings as though prodding his mistress forward. She could not hesitate any longer. Her path had been decided.

Skuld walked to the entrance of the cave, shaking loose the worry and fear with every step and replacing them with a single, driving thought. She would find the one responsible for this chaos, this fate-defying murderer and she would make them suffer.

Chapter Two: Niðavellir

The realm of the dwarves consisted of a dark and endless collection of caves. It started as a typical cave slanting down and inwards, but further down the air became sweltering and humid. That was the true sign you were among the dwarves; the heat from their forges permeated the air, making the very stones of the cave warm to the touch.

Skuld made her way further into the underground maze, trying to ignore the acrid metal tang that assaulted her nose and mouth. Along the way, she tamped down her inner doubts and the urge to turn back home by forcing one foot in front of the other.

She kept her sister's advice in the forefront of her mind. They traveled the realms before and so she trusted their advice. She wasn't naive enough to think she wouldn't be noticed, especially since her function as a Norn bound her to act if the fate of the realms became threatened. She just hoped she would recognize the important moments as they happened around her. It was easy to guide fate from afar. However when in the thick of it, could she do what was necessary to get destiny back on the correct path?

Strix cooed, breaking her out of her thoughts.

"You're right," Skuld responded to her companion. "There's no point in fretting. Things will work out the way they are supposed to." The words sounded hollow to her ears though.

The further she progressed along the rocky path, the wider the cave grew. Instead of becoming darker, the deeper she went the brighter it became. Strange luminescent moss covered the rock walls. In time, she heard the rush of water skimming over great falls and splashing into even bigger pools. The smell of green growing things hung in the air behind the musty odor of damp earth and heat from the forges deeper still.

"Who goes there?" a gravelly voice demanded, echoing against the cavern walls.

Skuld halted at the sound of the voice. "Who calls?" she countered.

Strix fluttered his wings and shifted his weight from one foot to another, still perched upon his mistress's shoulder.

A small boulder sat at the edge of the path shuddered and began transforming. As it grew taller, arms and legs sprouted from this rock-like formation, allowing it to tumble into the middle of the path in front of her.

Skuld squinted in the ambient light, attempting to make out the features suggested in the crevices of the stone. Two beady eyes, a bulbous nose, and a mouth covered by a generous beard became more and more apparent the longer she stared. At last, she realized the being addressing her was actually a dwarf disguised as a pile of stones.

"Which one are you?" Skuld asked, peering down at the short, squat dwarf. Her curiosity got the better of her as she wondered who would be the first creature she met.

Strix left her shoulder, flapping his wings until he perched on a nearby outcropping in the rock walls. There he could observe the exchange between his mistress and the creature without being in the way.

The dwarf raised his gray eyebrow in amusement. If

he noticed the owl's movement, he didn't pay it any attention. Instead, he addressed the woman before him. "I asked you first. You are a stranger here, not I."

Taken aback by his cold tone, Skuld replied confidently, "I will be a traveler and will have need of assistance." Wincing, she realized how strange she sounded. Why did tenses have to mess her up so much?

Shaking her head, she tried again. "I wish to speak with whichever one of you made this." She brought her left hand out from her cloak revealing the golden-hilted sword she'd tied to her belt. Ratatoskr's blood had dried giving the illusion of rust.

The dwarf's eyes widened at the sight of the sword. "Where did you get this?"

"You recognize this weapon?" Skuld took care to keep the blade just out of the creature's reach.

"Yes, I saw this very sword today, freshly forged, go to Dvalinn's daughters." The dwarf raised his gaze to the stranger. At the same time, he drew out a large war hammer from behind him and leveled it at her face. The words he uttered next were filled with unspoken threat. "It's impossible for you to have it now. I ask again, stranger, how did you come upon this sword?"

Skuld froze in place and blinked at the weapon being pointed at her. The promise of violence so soon after leaving home made her heart pound and her mind stop working. What about the rules of hospitality her sisters spoke of? Strangers were to be treated with respect. If they were not, it had to be taken as an insult. Whatever she did next, she could not allow herself to be perceived as weak.

Willing her arm not to shake with the weight of the sword, she brought the point up, angled to slice the dwarf's neck.

"This blade is what murdered a dear friend. Tell me who it is meant for, dwarf, or my friend will not be this sword's only victim today."

Abruptly, the dwarf brought his hammer up to deflect the sword tip away from him. Skuld lost her grip and the sword dropped to the ground. Panicking at being unarmed so soon, Skuld drew her dagger and etched a bind-rune in the air between her and her foe. The symbol flared brightly before vanishing.

"Witchcraft! Ha!" He cried out with derision even as he winced away from the brilliance. He tried to strike her with his hammer. But he remained motionless. Straining hard against what seemed to be invisible bonds, he fought to move even one finger.

Skuld grinned at the success of her spell. She maneuvered close enough behind him to press her dagger to his throat, just underneath his chest-length beard.

"I asked you nicely and you disrespected me. Last chance, maggot. Take me to the one who forged this sword or do I need to read the information in your entrails?" she hissed in his ear.

"I'm no maggot," the dwarf sputtered against the bite of the razor-sharp axe. "My name is Durin."

A wry smile played upon Skuld's lips as she recognized his name. "Ah, Durin. I might have guessed. Your name has revealed much. Don't you know the history of your species? You dwarves were formed out of the maggots infesting Ymir's rotting corpse."

The dwarf trembled in her arms. "Wh — who are you?"

Sensing her point had been received, Skuld took the dagger away from the dwarf's neck and moved back into his line of sight.

"I am no one to be trifled with. Take me to the dwarf who forged this sword." She bent to pick up the weapon that killed Ratatoskr before releasing the bind-rune to freeze him in place. "Be warned, Durin. Should you try to deceive me or run away, well, Strix here has an affinity for eyeballs. I am sure he will find yours quite delectable."

As if seconding Skuld's threat, Strix let out a loud screech, opened his wings, and launched himself from his perch. He dove straight for the dwarf, lightly scraping the top of his head with his outstretched talons as he passed by.

Shrieking with terror, Durin fell to the ground, his arms covering his head. "Alright! Alright! I will take you. Call off the bird."

Relieved at how easily she navigated her first social interaction with a realm-dweller, Skuld called out, "Strix. To me." The owl obeyed and returned to Skuld's shoulder.

"Lead the way, Durin," Skuld announced as she stroked the owl's chest. "There is no time to waste."

With much grumbling and mumbling under his breath, Durin rose to his feet and began walking down a hidden path Skuld would never have noticed on her own. "I will take you to Dvalinn, though I am not sure he will have the answers you seek."

"What do you mean?" Skuld requested.

"The weapon is a forgery," Durin spat. "Perhaps Dvalinn will know how it came to be in the first place." He waddled forward at an increased pace as though he wanted to leave the conversation behind.

"How is this a forgery? It's real enough to kill."

"It may kill, but I can assure you it's not the real thing. Believe me."

Skuld's eye narrowed. "How do you know? This was made by a dwarven hand. Now that I know who you are and who you are taking me to, I believe this to be the sword Týrfingr, a blade of significance in the Nine Realms, though I forget what for."

Durin whirled around, his fury overruling his fear for a brief moment. "How do I know that hunk of metal is a forgery? Dvalinn and I created the weapon you speak of together. We spent weeks crafting the sword. For me not to know every single inch of it is unthinkable. I don't know how a witch like you managed to get a replica of this caliber. Especially when the piece was completed mere hours ago. Something strange is going on here. So we are going to see Dvalinn. Let him figure this mess out."

Confused and suspicious, Skuld continued to follow the dwarf in silence.

They descended further into the cave. Eventually, the path widened enough to support two carts side by side. Piles of boulders and rocks lined the path. It took Skuld a few moments to realize these simple piles of stone were walls. Understanding that, she began to see the structure of the dwarven smithies.

Each had two tall standing walls to support the blazing forge. The rest of the space was corralled by shorter stone walls that came up to most dwarves' knees. Some draped a thin woven cloth from the stalagmites above to give the illusion of privacy, though those cloths were often singed and frayed at the edges. There were no doors into the smithies that Skuld could tell, just a gaping hole between stone piles. Large boulders served as workbenches off in the corners of the spaces while large intimidating iron anvils were centered in the middle of the one room. Marveling at the rudimentary architecture, Skuld wondered where the dwarves slept or if they lived and breathed metalsmithing so much that there wasn't time for anything else.

The further they walked the more dwarves Skuld saw. Most went about their lives, though a few of them eyed her as though they had never seen an outsider before. The heat from the forges made Skuld wish she could remove her traveling cloak. From the increased glares she received from passersby, she decided it would be best to remain as she was.

At last, they arrived at an impressive structure situated between five stalagmites. No ordinary metal smithy; it was easily three times the size of the other buildings around. Unlike those clumsy attempts at architecture, this had four complete walls reaching at least twenty feet in height. The stone edifices were smoothed and painted a deep blue. A large, round wooden door sat in the center and in the middle of the door sat a finely sculpted brass knocker etched with a knotted design.

"What is this place?" Skuld asked as they came to a halt in front of the building.

The dwarf squinted up at the structure. "This is the home of Dvalinn's daughters. They are holders of magic. They see what is coming and what has been. Dvalinn is here with the sword." With that, Durin made his way to the entrance, knocked the brass ring against the wood nine times and waited.

After a few moments, the door swung open, revealing a small, pale dwarf wearing a green dress with long braided brown hair and large brown eyes. Unlike Durin, she did not have a complexion of stone.

"Durin, welcome. Oh! I see you've brought a guest. Who might this be?" The female dwarf's voice was high pitched and didn't fit her homely features.

Durin ignored the question. "We need to see your father as soon as possible, Dilna. It's about our recent project."

The dwarf girl leveled her gaze upon Skuld as though she were trying to see into her heart, to read her intentions. The Norn remained still and quiet under the scrutiny, allowing Dilna to come to her own conclusions. Soon enough, the girl returned her attention to Durin.

As she and Durin discussed the need to interrupt Dvalinn, Skuld stood with her expression distant and aloof as she tried to remember anything in the runes she had carved about Dilna, Dvalinn's daughters, or even Dvalinn himself. Other than he and Durin were responsible for the forging of Týrfingr, the rest of their significance had been lost to her.

A sharp pinch from Strix's talons brought Skuld back to the present. Both the girl and Durin were staring at her, waiting for her to say something.

"I have need to speak with Dvalinn. I ask for help with this." Skuld twitched her cloak aside to reveal the sword.

The dwarf girl gasped. "Is that . . . ?"

Durin shook his head. "No, but now you see how important this is. Let us in."

Keeping her eyes on Skuld, the girl nodded reluctantly and stepped aside to allow them entrance. Once they were over the threshold, she closed the door.

Inside the building was not at all what Skuld expected. The entranceway opened up to an expansive and surprisingly well-lit room. Metal sconces along the walls held strong burning candles. Between the sconces hung intricate woven tapestries which shimmered in the flickering candlelight. The floor had been swept clean. A long rectangular fire pit raised about a foot off of the ground filled the center of the room. On one side, a cast-iron cauldron bubbled just above the embers, suspended by a long rail and hooks. An at once, a repulsive and mesmerizing aroma wafted from the concoction.

On the opposite end of the fire pit rested an odd arrangement of long, thin rectangular rocks that resembled sticks. There were dozens of them, their rough chiseled surfaces covered in soot and ash.

Placed around the pit were ten chairs covered in furs of all descriptions. A dais lifted each seat, raising whoever sat upon it higher than the normal dwarven visitor.

Against two opposite walls were two stone staircases spiraled up to what appeared to be a second floor. However, it wasn't a complete separation; the wooden boards supporting the rooms above had been cut in the middle exposing a rectangular hole right above the fire pit below.

"Wait here," the dwarf girl said. "I will get my sisters and my father." She scurried up the spiral staircase on the left, stealing glances back at Skuld as though the stranger were a puzzle she just couldn't piece together.

As they waited, Skuld sauntered around the room, feeling the imprint of the enchantments Dvalinn's daughters set up reverberating off of the very walls. It surprised her to feel the familiar resonance of the runes. The nine dwarven maids were powerful, though she could tell by the lingering energies they did not use the runes in the same ways she could.

She noted with interest that they seemed to focus on using the runes as charms or curses instead of to divine the future, heal, or their lesser-known applications in battle magic. The way the runes were applied to these curses was also unique to the dwarves. From inspecting the magically charged pile of stones in the fire pit, Skuld deduced the pieces stacked together like a puzzle to form the runes of the charm. As a result, the energies from their spell castings soaked into the stones, layering on top of the last like the ashes coating them.

Durin sat himself down on one of the benches, careful not to touch the nearest pelt covered chair. He watched the stranger and her owl poke around but didn't speak.

It wasn't long before the girl returned with her eight sisters and a grizzled looking dwarf who must have been Dvalinn.

The old dwarf roared, "Durin! What are you doing here? What mess have you brought into my home?"

Skuld stepped forward before Durin could reply. "I will come to find out more about this weapon. Where will it go when it leaves your forge? Do you know what happens to it when it will be lost?" She held out the blood-encrusted blade and dropped it before the gathering of dwarves. It clattered onto the stone floor.

Dvalinn scoffed and eight of his daughters tittered amongst themselves. The only one who took the situation seriously was the youngest daughter, Dilna, who watched Skuld like a hawk.

"She sounds crazy, yes, but it looks exactly like Týrfingr," Durin interjected. "If I didn't know any better, I'd swear it's the same sword myself."

Durin's words cut Dvalinn's chuckle short. Wordlessly he bent down to pick up the weapon. It stood a head taller than the dwarf, but he handled it with dexterous ease. He inspected the blade, turning the aged iron over in his gnarled, weathered hands with care. He took his time inspecting the metal, the craftsmanship, and all of the little secrets he learned to look for in worked metal.

Anger replaced confusion on Dvalinn's expression. In a low, glowering voice, he told Skuld, "I don't know what kind of witch you are, but I will not have this elvish abomination in my home. This is not Týrfingr and I will not have my time wasted any more. Leave now! You are not welcome here, stranger."

Skuld's mouth dropped open at the abruptness of her dismissal. It made her cheeks flush with heat and her blood boil. "You would dare violate your own rules of hospitality? I have come to you for help."

Dvalinn didn't back down from her challenge. He puffed up his chest and stood tall against her threats. "You heard me, witch. I'll not give you the help you seek. You are not welcome here. You're probably a spy from those damn elves or worse the Vanir. They know the elves are inferior smiths. Did they send you to spy on our methods and to confound us with replicas of weapons we are making? Did they?"

The accusations made little sense to her; Skuld tried to understand why it would matter. "I will not know what you are talking about," she replied. "I am not a Vanir goddess."

"I doubt you'd admit it if you were," Dvalinn said. "This war between the Æsir and the Vanir is going to happen, and we dwarves are backing the Æsir. You can tell those damned elves to mind their business." He shoved the older, ill-kempt, and dirty Týrfingr at her, causing Skuld to take an involuntary step backward

Dvalinn motioned to his daughters to follow him back up the steps. They all lined up and followed their father, casting her disdainful glares at the Norn along the way. All, that is, except Dilna, who stayed near the bottom of the stairs.

Before Dvalinn disappeared to the upper reaches of the building, he paused to call down, "It occurs to me with this war coming, it is best to be cautious. A dead spy can't tell any secrets. I've changed my mind. Girls, kill her." After uttering his demand, he disappeared from sight.

Dvalinn's daughters all peered at her from their places scattered over the staircase and the upper floor over the railing. A strange glint sparkled in their eyes.

Furious at being threatened and denied answers on top of having precious time wasted, Skuld stood to her full height and glared back at them. She had only asked for help which, according to their customs, they were honor-bound to give her. If Dvalinn wanted to threaten her life, then she would make sure he and his daughters regret it.

As her anger mounted, the dwarven girls began to stomp their wide, bare feet on the stone steps. The force of their combined effort made the building rumble. Their dance leveled out into a strange, staccato rhythm. It made the very air thrum with energy.

The reverberations sent a chill of recognition through Skuld's neck. Whatever they were doing, they were calling on the power of the runes. A sudden movement out of the corner of her eye made her head whip around to the fire pit on her left. The rocks which caught her attention before tumbled around, stacking and unstacking themselves at a rapid pace.

Skuld grabbed for her dagger and etched a protective bind-rune around herself just before a blast of fire erupted from the magically manipulated rocks. The flames engulfed her. She grit her teeth against the heat, hoping her skin would not get blistered from this ostentatious manner of cursing. It seemed the dwarfish techniques of shaping metal extended to the creation of their magic. The flames were not meant to kill her outright, rather the fire carried whatever curse the dwarven sisters aimed at her.

As the fire subsided, she sensed the lingering energy of their curse grate against her bind-rune shield as though looking for a crack in her spell. For a brief moment, Skuld wondered if the people of the realms could harm her. She always assumed because of her and her sisters' closeness to the eternal Yggdrasil they were immune to death. But what if they were vulnerable in the realms?

As Skuld's doubts grew, so too did her determination. Her sisters had been right; showing weakness was dangerous in the realms. In order to survive and save Yggdrasil, she had to show no mercy. Starting with these dwarves.

She heard the click-clacking of the stones rearranging themselves and the pounding of dwarven feet. Another curse came.

With swift, dexterous moves, Skuld drew a hasty assemblage of runes against the shield that protected her. As the rune stones stopped moving, she braced herself for another burst of flame. The moment the fire touched her protective shield, it shattered and exploded outward with the violence of a winter storm. The icy blast extinguished the fire while simultaneously expelling the dwarven curses back to where they came from.

The maids shrieked and ducked to avoid the shards

of ice hurtling at them.

Before they could regroup, Skuld dashed to the fire pit and carved a counter-curse over the spell-soaked puzzle rocks.

"What are you doing?" Screamed one of the maidens, both outraged and terrified.

Skuld ignored her and kept her focus on her task. It took time, but the glow of Skuld's runes ate away at the stone, crumbling them to no more than gray dust.

"Durin, stop her!" another maid shrieked.

Durin stepped towards Skuld.

"Touch me and your eyes will be forfeit," Skuld reminded him.

Strix flapped his wings and screeched. Durin backed away and hastily covered his head with his hands.

When she was sure they would not attack again, Skuld picked up the sword she brought and headed for the door. She exited the building and Durin followed just out of striking distance.

Mindful of the danger of lingering, she paused at the threshold. Holding her dagger aloft, she etched some runes into the soft, pliant wood of the door.

"What are you doing?" Durin demanded. "You shouldn't be doing that. Stop it!"

Skuld ignored him and continued focusing on the runes. When she finished, the sigils she wrote on the door flared with a bright light before fading back to nothing.

Her work done, Skuld turned to Durin. "Are you going to answer any of my questions?"

Casting a worried glance upwards as though Dvalinn would pop out and yell at him at any moment, Durin shook his head. "No, I will not. You need to leave. Leave Niðavellir. Dvalinn was right; you don't belong here. I made a mistake letting you in."

Her blue eyes met Durin's brown ones and held his gaze for a long moment. She said in a deep, ominous voice of warning, "Should you follow me, you will regret it even more than you will for not helping me."

Durin gaped after her.

As she traveled back through the caverns, Skuld mulled over the situation. The sword was an exact replica of Týrfingr. How could it be possible? What replica could even compare to a dwarf-forged sword? They were the best smiths in all the Nine Realms. They were masters at metalsmithing. No one in the Nine Realms could even come close to their craftsmanship.

Then where did her sword come from? How could it have been confused with the Týrfingr that had just been made even by the dwarves who made it?

Unless the dwarves had made both weapons. A tingling of an idea began forming in the back of her mind. What if her sword wasn't a replica? What if it was the same as the other one, but from a different time?

Would it even be possible?

Skuld chewed on her lip as she continued walking, turning over the theory in her mind. Perhaps her sisters would know more about how such a thing could happen.

"Wait!" a shrill voice called out from behind her. "Wait a moment, please!"

Skuld turned to see Dilna, the little dwarf maid, running after her. "What do you want?" she asked coldly.

Panting, the dwarf girl skidded to a halt a few feet away from the Norn. The maid gulped for air, winded from her sprint. Between her ragged breaths, she panted, "You laid a curse on our home. What will it do?"

Arching her eyebrow, Skuld answered, "An inhospitable host has no need for a home. For every creature who crosses the threshold and your family does not help, then the home will fall, little by little. The damage will last; no repairs will fix what offenses have wrought."

The maid shook her head, repentant. "I am sorry for how my father treated you. I am sorry my sisters tried to curse you. However, you should know those rules haven't been observed by our kind in generations. No one but the Æsir and a few needy humans ever tread into our realm. But you, you are different. You're a vǫlva, a seer like me, aren't you?"

The hope in her voice exasperated Skuld. "Not like you but similar enough. What of it?"

"The human who commissioned the sword Týrfingr is known as Svafrlami. Except he didn't ask politely. He tricked my father and Durin and forced them to make the weapon. My sisters and I cursed the blade today. We finished the spell not long before Durin brought you to our home."

Dilna's flood of information caused Skuld to kneel to eye level with the dwarf maid. "Cursed? How did you curse the blade?"

Dilna wrung her hands together, trying not to make eye contact with the stranger. "Svafrlami will get the sword he asked for — one that would never miss a stroke, would never rust, and would cut through iron and stone as easily as through cloth. Týrfingr will also kill a man each time it is drawn from its sheath and it will be the cause of three great evils before it is lost to history."

Skuld regarded the old, battered sword, impressed by the thoroughness of the dwarven maids' work. "Is this the same sword you and your sisters cursed?" She handed it to the dwarf.

Dilna accepted the sword by the tarnished golden hilt. She inspected it, feeling out with her powers to sense the traces of a curse left on the metal. At the corners of her sight, a soft glow appeared along the edges of the blade with a familiar warmth and a familiar light. Gasping, Dilna dropped the hilt as though it burned.

Doing her best to hide her smirk, Skuld picked up the sword. "Well? Is it the same sword?"

The dwarf blinked and nodded. "I — I don't know how, but it is the same."

Skuld nodded. "Tell me Dilna, what are the three great evil deeds you and your sisters will curse Týrfingr to do?"

Dilna shrugged her shoulders. "I don't know. We did not specify what the deeds were. It is left to the Nornir to decide. Perhaps they have to do with the coming war between the Æsir and the Vanir."

Skuld pursed her lips. "Perhaps. I know how to find out for sure." She rose to her feet. "Thank you, Dilna." She turned to walk away, to continue her journey out of Niðavellir. There was much she needed to consult with her sisters about.

"Wait. What about your curse?"

"What about it?"

"I thought if I told you what you wanted to know you would reverse it?"

The very request irritated Skuld. "You want me to remove my curse? After your father disrespected my plea for help and ordered my death? Do you know what I am, Dilna?"

The dwarf maid shook her head.

"I am a Norn, one of the three sisters who determine the fates of all in Yggdrasil. If I wanted I could uncarve the fate of you and all of your sisters. I could erase you from existence."

Dilna trembled at the words and, with wide eyes, she shook her head. "Please," she whispered.

"I will not do that. However, the curse on your home will remain. Perhaps it will help to bring back the rules of hospitality to your people once again."

Without looking back at the chest-fallen maiden, Skuld walked resolutely back up the path.

The hike up took longer than the journey down. Skuld, who climbed high into the branches of Yggdrasil had to stop and catch her breath more times than she wanted to admit. With her legs burning, she came to the cave opening.

"We are almost home, Strix," she murmured.

The owl stretched his wings, eager to be back where he could fly freely.

Skuld walked through the opening, expecting to see the familiar terrain of Yggdrasil. Instead, a vast and bitter cold world of ice and snow awaited her. A stiff, frozen wind pierced her skin even through her clothing. The cold stung her eyes so fiercely she could barely make out the snow-covered landscape surrounding her. Bare limbed trees sparsely dotted the rocks and storm clouds obscured the vague shadowy outlines of mountains in the far distance.

Strix buried his head against the nape of his mistress's neck, using her hair as a shield against the ice.

"This isn't Yggdrasil. Where are we?" Skuld asked, straining to keep her eyes open against the sleet. Wondering if she took a wrong turn, she glanced back to the cave. Panic shot through her when the entrance couldn't be found. In fact, no hint a cave ever existed remained.

Skuld fought against her mounting fear while scrambling for what to do. In a matter of moments, her boots and her clothes were soaked through from the deep snow, chilling her to her very bones. What was this? Why was it so cold? Where was her home?

At once a loud roar overpowered the sound of the wind, causing her to jump and look wildly around for the source of the noise. Another deafening crash sounded, this time accompanied by the distinct clacking of rocks colliding against each other and a slow, gritty static of snow sliding down a hill. Skuld whipped her head around to the mountainside behind her. Just through the flurries of snow, she saw a rush of white peppered with the dark rocks sliding towards her, building into an ever louder hiss.

With terror in her heart, Skuld made a break for what appeared to be the base of the mountain she stood on.

Strix took to the air, but struggled to keep up with his mistress because of the harsh wind and blinding sleet.

Running in the thick covering of snow proved to be more difficult than Skuld imagined. She hiked her knees high, trying to lift her feet out of the slush, but it piled too high.

The sounds of the avalanche grew louder with each step she took. The realization she wasn't going to make it to safety infuriated and terrified her.

Out of the storm, a figure collided into Skuld's side, sending her careening towards a large pile of boulders. Unable to control her legs, she toppled into the snow just short of the potential shelter. Someone grabbed hold of her cloak and dragged her through the ice towards the boulders just as the initial wave of the avalanche arrived.

All Skuld saw were blurs of white and black. The spray of snow and small pebbles came at her fast. Through sheer will, she kept her eyes squeezed shut and covered her face against the burning cold and sting of rocks. Inside she panicked. If she hadn't gotten back to her home in Yggdrasil, then where in the Nine Realms was she?

Chapter Three: The Valkyrie

The avalanche seemed to last for an eternity and mere moments simultaneously. The sliding river of ice, sleet, and rocks slowed and then stopped altogether. The boulder she and her mysterious savior huddled behind forced the snow to go around it creating a pocket of relative safety. Skuld turned her head to look at the person who rescued her and was confronted by the sight of what appeared to be a human, but with more feathers than they were supposed to have.

"Who are you?" Skuld asked as she wondered if she should be concerned about the feathers.

The figure mumbled through the thick layers. "You're welcome for saving you."

Skuld wasn't sure how to respond, so she didn't say anything.

By the sound of the voice, it was a female, though you wouldn't be able to tell by the many layers of clothing and what looked to be a fluttering cape of white feathers. A thick bundle of branches and twigs lay beside the figure.

"This is like no place I've ever been to before. On my way back to camp from getting the firewood, the storm blew in quicker than any winter squall I've seen. It's lucky I spotted you when I did. You would have been crushed by the avalanche. Oh, my name is Brynhildr," her mysterious savior answered the initial question as though it were an afterthought.

The name tickled a distant memory for Skuld. "Brynhildr," she repeated, straining to remember why the name seemed so familiar. The importance of the person balanced just on the tip of her memory, but the feathered cape snapping in the wind that made the connection for her. "You will be the Valkyrie Brynhildr?"

Valkyries were known as Choosers of the Slain; female warriors hand-picked by the Æsir god Óðinn and set to the task of selecting the best human warriors who died in battle and bring them to Valhǫll, in Ásgarðr to join his army. They flew over battlefields in Miðgarðr with their swan-suits to take the souls of the slain. Óðinn wanted the best to fight with him come Ragnarǫk — the epic battle that always signaled the end of the realm-cycle.

Valkyries weren't uncommon in and of themselves, but Brynhildr's name stood out in Skuld's mind for some reason. If only she could ask the runes why!

"Yes, one and the same. Have we met before?"

"I'm Skuld," the Norn answered despite herself. "You and I will know each other soon."

The bundled figure tilted her head to the side. "What an odd thing to say."

Skuld flushed with embarrassment. Cursed tenses!

Brynhildr didn't make any more mention of the Norn's error. "Well, it seems the danger has passed. Come on, Skuld. I have a shelter over here. Maybe we can figure out how to get out of this place together."

Brynhildr hefted the bundle of twigs up and motioned with her head for the Norn to follow and started trudging through the knee-deep snow.

Resigning herself, she followed the Valkyrie's footsteps.

Strix hooted his relief at his mistress' safety before alighting upon her shoulder.

Brynhildr made quite an impressive shelter

underneath a sharp outcropping of rocks and a few boulders covering the opening except for a small gap near the ground. The amount of strength that feat must have taken was more than any human could muster with their own two hands. It made Skuld wonder who made this alcove before Brynhildr happened upon it.

Inside the makeshift tent of stone, a campfire had recently gone out. Smoke tendrils enveloped a crude, hastily made spit with a rabbit impaled on it. A small pile of evergreen twigs piled near the boulder gave the small space a pervading aroma of pine intermingling with cooking meat.

After adding the branches she brought to the existing pile, the Valkyrie settled herself next to the fire pit. Taking the time to unravel the elaborate wrappings that covered her head and face, she let out a sigh as she shook free a mane of red-gold hair. She had a classical sort of beauty with piercing blue eyes that could see right through to the very marrow of a person. She was also very young; no more than thirteen winters and not far along her path as a Valkyrie from what Skuld could tell.

With her face free, Brynhildr began the tedious task of starting the fire again.

Skuld sat on the opposite side of the fire and watched as Brynhildr blew on the fading embers, coaxing the flame back to life.

It took a certain amount of grit to be a Valkyrie. The title was traditionally bestowed upon the fiercest of Shield Maidens. Óðinn commanded a large army of these warrior women of all races and all kinds. The All-Father did not discriminate, however, these Shield Maidens were older than Brynhildr. Typically the oath binding these women to Óðinn's service lasted for a year and a day. After, they were free to do as they chose; either relinquish their Valkyrie position and live the rest of their lives or continue for another year and a day presiding over the fiercest battles and watching an everlasting vista of carnage.

At last, the fire caught and the heat from the flames began to warm the inside of the shelter. Brynhildr patiently fed the flames twigs until it grew big enough for some of the larger pieces.

Aching for the warmth, Skuld scooted closer to the fire as Strix fluttered to the pile of pine branches. The heat from the flames made her frozen fingers tingle as feeling returned to them. She brushed the ice from her clothes and shook the snow out of her dark hair.

"Where were you before appearing here?" Brynhildr asked as she prodded at the rabbit on the spit with her fingers.

"Niðavellir," Skuld answered before she could think of anything else to say.

Brynhildr laughed. "That's a new one. Haven't heard of anyone visiting the dwarves before."

"Well, their hospitality is lacking, so I wouldn't recommend going."

"Good to know," the Valkyrie smirked. She withdrew a dagger from her belt and sliced off a piece of the rabbit to offer to Skuld. The Norn accepted the meat, tore the piece in half, and offered some to Strix. The owl flitted from the pine branches to the ground next to his mistress, accepting the offering of rabbit. Skuld nibbled at her portion, tasting it with caution. The texture felt somewhere between chewy and charred with a gamey flavor she found rather unappealing. She should have brought some of the berries from Yggdrasil in her pack.

A howling wind pushed in a frigid breeze through the seams of the boulders and the rock face. Skuld hunched closer to the flames, trying to angle away from the reminders of the cold. After giving the rest of the meat to Strix, she asked, "How did you get here?"

Brynhildr finished chewing her piece of rabbit. She seemed unconcerned with the thunder and sleet coming down. "Well, I was flying to Valhǫll and somehow blown off course. I blinked and all of a sudden I found myself in the middle of a blizzard bearing down on me. I did what I could to get some sort of shelter together. It's so strange to have a blizzard this late in the spring. The storm lets up for a little bit, but then it comes back with a vengeance when I try to find a way out. Near as I can tell, I've been here for a day, maybe two." She regarded the new arrival, sizing her up and trying to come to a conclusion about her. At last, she blurted out, "You're not human, are you?"

Skuld blinked. "What do you mean?"

"Don't be coy. Anyone with eyes can see you are not. Humans don't have runes in their eyes or on their fingernails. Are you Æsir? Vanir? Maybe Elvish? Tell me."

Skuld considered how to respond. Her sisters told her people of the realms feared them and fear could be difficult to predict. What's more, for some reason she didn't want this human to fear her, not yet. Though she couldn't quite pinpoint why. At last, she settled with, "I am what I am."

Brynhildr narrowed her eyes. "Well, aren't you mysterious? Say, what kind of a name is Skuld? Not human, that's for sure."

"It's my name, no more and no less." Skuld wrapped her arms around her knees and stared at the fire, not wanting to meet Brynhildr's gaze.

The girl pursed her lips in thought as she pulled out a drinking horn with a wooden stopper in the top. After removing the stopper, she offered it to Skuld. "Mead?"

Skuld accepted the horn and took a swig. The sweet, fermented liquid made her tongue tingle. Passing the horn back to the Valkyrie, she asked, "Do you know how long the storm will last?"

Brynhildr shrugged and took a sip herself. "Never can tell. We are stuck here until it passes so we might as well make ourselves comfortable." She settled her back against one of the stone walls. "Why were you in Niðavellir anyway? What could you want with the dwarves?" She handed the horn back to Skuld.

"My business is my own." The sentence came out terser than Skuld intended. She took another drink of the mead. It warmed her a bit, despite the tingling sensation.

Brynhildr held up her hands in defeat. "Alright then. What shall we talk about? Since you don't want to talk about yourself, you can decide the topic."

"Why do we need to talk?"

"I don't want to just sit here in silence. We don't know how long this storm is going to last. And when it ends, we still have to find a way out of this frozen place. Like it or not, we are stuck together. It might be nice to know a little about each other, don't you think?" Brynhildr took the horn back and drank a long swig from it. When she finished, she gave the skeptical Norn a lopsided grin. "I have an idea. Since you don't want to talk, why don't we play taflkast? You don't have a problem with dice games, do you?"

Confusion found its way past Skuld's guarded features. "Dice? What is dice?"

The human woman sputtered out a laugh. "You don't know what dice are? By the gods, how long were you with the dwarves? No, I take it back. Even those miserable blacksmiths know what fun is."

"What are you talking about?" Skuld's irritation deepened.

The Valkyrie held up a hand, indicating for Skuld to wait. Her other hand untied a leather pouch attached to her belt. Withdrawing a couple of rectangular pieces of bone, she held them out to the strange woman sitting across the fire from her. "These are dice. The idea is to cast them onto a flat surface. You can't let your opponent see what combination you rolled. They will ask you what it is. You can either tell them the truth or you can lie. However, if your opponent calls your bluff, then you lose points."

"Points?"

"It's how you can tell who wins. If your opponent doesn't call your bluff on what you cast, then you earn a point. The player who has the most points after nine rounds wins."

Skuld took the bone dice, rolling them between her fingers and her palm. They were lighter than she expected, the bone worn smooth except for the dots which punctured each side of the cubed design. "What do they win?"

Brynhildr thought for a moment. "Let's say the winner gets a favor from the other person sometime in the future? How does that sound?"

The Norn considered the offer. "Alright then. Who shall go first?"

"Why don't you go first," the Valkyrie suggested.

Nodding, Skuld slammed her hand with the dice down on the ground, trapping the bone pieces underneath her palm.

Brynhildr laughed, "Not like that. Here, let me show you." She scooted closer to Skuld and touched her hand to remove the dice from beneath them.

Skuld jumped at the feel of the Valkyrie's hand.

Brynhildr ignored the reaction. "Like this, watch." She shook the bone dice in her lightly closed fist three times before tossing them to the ground. "See? You try."

Brynhildr picked up the objects and set them into Skuld's palm, closing the woman's fingers around them. She released Skuld's hand and sat back to wait. As she waited, she ripped a leg off of the rabbit on the spit and took a large bite.

Hesitantly, Skuld repeated the motions. The dice rolled on the ground with a dull clatter. Skuld covered the dice so Brynhildr wouldn't see what she had rolled.

"So? What did you roll?"

She peeked under her hand. "There are eight dots showing."

"You're lying," Brynhildr said from around a

mouthful of rabbit without hesitating.

Skuld frowned. "You are correct. I suppose you get the point?"

"Those are the rules. Now it's my turn to roll." Brynhildr took up the dice and let them tumble out of her hand. They landed off to her right side, away from Skuld's eager gaze.

"Well? How many dots do the dice show?" the Norn asked.

"There are five dots."

Skuld looked intently at Brynhildr's stoic facial features, trying to discern whether or not she told the truth. At last, she pronounced, "You are bluffing."

Trying to hide her smirk, Brynhildr handed the dice back to Skuld. "You are correct. We are tied in points." As Skuld shook the dice in her hand and before she let them roll onto the ground, the Valkyrie spoke up. "Why don't we make this more interesting? Let's say the winner of the round can ask the loser any question and the loser has to answer it. What do you say?"

Skuld rolled her eyes. "Why are you so intent on talking?"

The young Valkyrie shrugged good-naturedly. "I can't help it. I'm curious by nature. Come on, it's boring otherwise."

Skuld heaved a sigh and cast a furtive glance outside. The wind still howled and ice and snow still arched in frantic flurries. There was no sign of the storm letting up yet and so no chance for her to keep going with her mission. "Fine."

Brynhildr clapped her hands together in childish delight. "Wonderful! Here, it's your turn!" She pushed the dice over to her opponent, her grin plastered on her face and her blue eyes shining in the firelight.

"I don't know why you are so happy about this," Skuld said. "It is just a guessing game."

"I'm happy because I like meeting new and

interesting people."

"Who says I am interesting?"

"I can just tell."

"Is that why you became a Valkyrie? Because of all the people you'd get to meet as they die in battle?"

Brynhildr ignored the intended barb and shook her finger at her, the smile still glued to her face. "Ah, ah, ah. No questions unless you win a round. That's the deal."

Skuld made a face at being scolded and rolled the dice. After a brief glance at the results, she covered them with her hand and waited for Brynhildr to ask.

"What did you roll?" Brynhildr still smiled as though the questions she held inside were about to come bursting forth with or without her consent.

"Eleven," Skuld answered, being sure to stare her straight in the eye.

"I call your bluff," Brynhildr said.

Frowning, Skuld removed her hand from atop the dice. Nine dots faced her. "I suppose you have a question already?" She sighed as she handed over the dice.

The Valkyrie practically bounced up and down with excitement. "I have dozens. But as per our agreement, I will only ask one."

"Get it over with," Skuld settled so her back rested against one of the boulders that formed the side of the makeshift shelter. Her arms crossed over her chest as she waited.

"I know you said you'd been in Niðavellir, but where do you come from? Where is your home?"

Skuld told her matter-of-factly, "Yggdrasil."

Brynhildr expelled a groan. "That's not an answer. We are all from Yggdrasil. Tell me where you're really from."

"I did tell you. And it's one question per turn."

"Alright then, I'll roll." Once again, the dice tumbled to the ground. Brynhildr covered up the results. "It's nine."

"I think you are bluffing."

A satisfied grin appeared on the Valkyrie's face. She revealed the dice in a flourish. Indeed, one had four dots and the other five. "That means I get to ask you another question."

A heavy sigh escaped Skuld's lips. "Fine. What is your question?"

"What were you doing with the dwarves in Niðavellir?"

Gritting her teeth, Skuld studied Brynhildr's expectant face. It became obvious the young Valkyrie wasn't going to let the subject go. If she were honest with herself, Skuld would admit to being curious as to what sort of life this young girl would lead. Since the past was not her strong suit, she decided to forward into Brynhildr's future. Before she told her secrets, she wanted to see what choices this vivacious Valkyrie would make and determine what sort of person she would become.

Taking out her obsidian dagger, Skuld focused on Brynhildr's face and carved the runes to show her fate surreptitiously into the earth next to her.

"Hey, what's that?" Brynhildr strained her neck to see what the Norn was doing.

Skuld didn't hear her as she fixated on what the runes showed her.

Colors slid around in a kaleidoscope pattern around the sigils and rushed past the Norn as she peered into the future. Static and abrupt, the images shifted rapidly and did not show as much information as they should have. Pictures of a sleeping warrior in armor came to the forefront. A ring of cursed fire barricaded the prone figure. A strapping silhouette on a mighty stallion leaps over the blaze. His blonde curls reflect the dancing flames as he approaches the armor-clad person. He removes the armor with care revealing none other than Brynhildr's sleeping face. He kisses her and her eyes flutter open.

Time skids forward to another young man who approaches a stone keep situated on a different hill. He wears another's face as an illusion. Deception, betrayal. False marriages and murder. Fierce, burning anger and depthless sorrow until a long wagon ride into the depths of Niflheimr, bound for Hel.

"Hey, come on now," Brynhildr's voice brought Skuld's awareness back to the present. "You have to answer. That's the rules of the game."

Still reeling from all she had seen, Skuld blinked, reconciling what the strangely chaotic visions meant. This Brynhildr was one of importance in the realms. At least for now. If Skuld wasn't careful in her interactions with this girl, she could upset the balance even more. Wordlessly, she smeared the runes away and thought about how much to reveal.

After a long moment, Skuld admitted, "I'm looking for someone and I thought the dwarves could help me."

The Valkyrie blinked in surprise. "The dwarves? But they don't venture very far from their caverns. How could they have helped you find anyone?"

Lifting the edges of her damp cloak, Skuld revealed the sword Týrfingr at her side. "They forged this weapon. I thought they could tell me more about it."

Brynhildr eyed the sword. "Is that blood?"

Skuld shrugged, still hesitant to fully trust her. "I didn't put it there."

Sensing Skuld wasn't quite ready to relinquish all of her secrets, Brynhildr handed over the dice. "Your turn."

Pursing her lips, Skuld accepted the dice and shook them in both hands before allowing them to tumble to the ground. Barely glancing at the number, she covered the results with her hand. "Seven," she said, keeping her voice neutral.

The human girl studied the Norn. Brynhildr knew she lied on account of the dice being weighted, but she also sensed that if Skuld lost again things would not go very well. In the interest of keeping the peace, she said, "I believe you."

The wide smile which broke out on Skuld's face lit up her features like the ethereal lights in the northern night sky. "Ha!" she exclaimed as she brandished the results of her roll. "I lied! I win this time! I get to ask you a question now."

Brynhildr hadn't expected such an exuberant response. She smiled, willing to let the strange woman ask what she wished. "What do you want to ask me then?"

Skuld leaned forward, her eyes intent on the girl's face. "You're very young. Swearing the oath to Óðinn is done by women who have seen their first moon blood. You haven't reached womanhood yet."

Brynhildr shifted uncomfortably. It wasn't a topic she wanted to discuss with a stranger. More than a little defensive, she asked, "Is there a question?"

Skuld ignored the sass and leaned in closer to the girl. "Why will Óðinn allow you to take the oath to become one of his Choosers of the Slain?"

The way Skuld asked the question set Brynhildr's teeth on edge. However, fair was fair. If the Valkyrie wanted to get more information out of the mysterious woman then she'd have to give up some of her story as well.

After a long, considering pause, Brynhildr said, "My brother, Atli. He trained me since I could walk to be a Shield Maiden. It's true I've yet to see my moon blood, but I've already seen my fair share of death. When I reached ten years of age, Atli promised me to Óðinn. He thought there would be no greater honor than to have a Valkyrie for a sister. Óðinn agreed. That was three winters ago."

As she handed over the dice, Skuld considered what Brynhildr told her. "So you live with the gods in Ásgarðr?"

A smirk appeared on the young Valkyrie's face. "You'll have to win the next round if you want the answer to that." She rolled the dice, taking extra care to examine the results she knew would be there. "I rolled an eight."

But now Skuld had the confidence in the game. "You're bluffing," she said. Without even bothering to look at the revealed dice, she demanded, "Answer my question."

"No, I do not live in Ásgarðr. I live with my brother in Miðgarðr on a mountain called Hindarfjall, though he is rarely home. I have the keep to myself most of the time. When Óðinn sends the call for his Valkyries, I don my swan suit and fly to battle. That's the only time I see the All-Father." She lifted the cape of white feathers as evidence. She fed a few more twigs into the fire. "I think he is preparing for the coming war with the Vanir." She paused, a twig halfway into the flames, and regarded the woman warily. "You're not one of them, are you?"

"What? Vanir?" Skuld blinked. Why did so many ask that question? "No, I am not."

Brynhildr nodded, accepting the answer. "I didn't think so. I know you aren't human. Beyond that, I am not quite sure what you are." Noting Skuld's gaze shift down to the fire, Brynhildr mused out loud, "I suppose I have no choice but to win the information from you."

The Norn did her best to hide her smile. This game was fun, so why not continue? Truth be told, without her sisters, Skuld felt empty and lonely. She'd never been away from them or their home near the well for so long before. This game with Brynhildr lessened the homesickness and it was good to talk with someone.

She brought her gaze up again to meet Brynhildr's. In a serious tone, she said, "If you guess what number I roll on this next turn, I will tell you what you want to know. However, if you do not correctly guess, that will be the end of it. We will not bring up the subject of who or what I am again."

"Deal," Brynhildr agreed. She stuck out her hand towards Skuld, intending to shake on the bargain.

Skuld eyed the offered hand. "What are you doing?"

"We made a deal. We seal the bargain by shaking hands."

Skuld held out her hand similar to how Brynhildr had hers. Uncertainly, she wiggled her fingers in the air. "Like this?"

Laughing, the Valkyrie replied, "No. Here, like this." She grasped Skuld's hand, palm to palm, and then raised and dropped her arm three times in succession. "There, the bargain has been struck. We can't go back on it." She released Skuld's hand.

Stretching her fingers from the Valkyrie's warm touch, Skuld frowned. Such an odd ritual. Why wouldn't the words bind the oath? Humans were strange creatures, and this young one doubly so.

Brynhildr handed over the dice to her strange companion. "Roll the dice."

"Alright." Skuld let the dice fall from her palm and, after taking a cursory glance at the results, covered them with her hands. She waited for Brynhildr to proclaim her guess.

Without removing her gaze from Skuld's eyes, Brynhildr answered with complete confidence, "Nine."

Surprise and shock registered on the Norn's face. "H—how did you know?"

"I have magic all my own," Brynhildr joked, a wide smile on her face. "Now tell me, mysterious Skuld, who and what are you?"

Heaving a sigh, Skuld tried to find the right way to explain. She wasn't sure she could make Brynhildr comprehend. She didn't even know if humans were aware of the existence of her and her sisters, so seldom did they venture out into Miðgarðr. The only creature to visit them was Óðinn when he performed his self-sacrifice. However, that hadn't yet occurred in this cycle.

"One day, Óðinn will come to the branches of Yggdrasil and sacrifice himself to earn the powers of the runes."

Brynhildr's eyebrows scrunched together in confusion. "Óðinn does not use rune magic."

Skuld suppressed a smile. "He will."

"What does this have to do with who and what you are?"

Ignoring the question, Skuld continued. "After Óðinn hangs himself on Yggdrasil for nine nights, my sisters and I will pull his dying body from the branches of the World Tree and bring him back to health. As we will do, we whisper to him secrets of the runes and the powers they possess. He sought knowledge and who will we be to deny him after he'd sacrificed himself for it? In order to fulfill the part he needs to play in the Nine Realms, he will have need of the wisdom of the runes to do it."

The human made an expression of disbelief. "Are you telling me you are one of the Wyrd Sisters?"

Skuld sat up straight and lifted her chin. "I am. We care for Yggdrasil and we carve the fates of the Nine Realms into its bark."

"I thought there were more than just three of you," Brynhildr said. "I was taught everyone has one and depending on what kind of life they lead, they either have a happy Norn or a miserable Norn."

"That is absurd." Skuld shook her head. "No, there are only three of us. We are responsible for what was, what is, and what should be."

"What you are saying is impossible."

"Impossible or not, I have told you the truth. Whether you believe or not is your concern, not mine." Skuld brushed off the disbelief, though Brynhildr's denial hurt her more than she cared to admit.

Brynhildr crossed her arms over her chest. "Alright then, what are you doing here in the Nine Realms instead of at the Well of Destiny?"

"I told you. I am looking for someone."

"No, I mean why are you stuck here? Shouldn't you be able to just pop in and out of all the realms at will? Why did I have to save you from an avalanche and tear my swan suit in the process?"

Brynhildr's questions stung Skuld's pride and without thinking, she lashed out. "I could ask the same of you, Valkyrie. Why didn't you fly towards Ásgarðr when the storm broke? You had time before the avalanche and before the storm returned. Why are you ignoring Óðinn's summons?"

Brynhildr's confused and suspicious expression turned to a deep glower. "Are you suggesting I am shirking my duties as a Valkyrie?" The menace in Brynhildr's cheerful voice became razor sharp. "That I am a coward? Choose your words carefully, Skuld. You will not be able to take them back once they are past your teeth."

Skuld didn't heed the warning in the human's tone. "I'm suggesting there's more to you being here than simply waiting for a storm to pass. As a Valkyrie, you should have been able to outfly a simple blizzard. Perhaps you are too weak-willed. Or maybe you aren't really a Valkyrie at all. Perhaps you stole that swan skin from one of your betters."

The fury with which Brynhildr glared at Skuld could have withered a lesser person. "I've killed people for insinuating less," Brynhildr threatened darkly. "How dare you insult my integrity!"

Skuld tossed Brynhildr her pair of dice. "Perhaps you are not as suited for being a Valkyrie as your brother thinks."

Brynhildr scowled at the strange woman, debating on whether or not to make her regret her words. Norn or not, Brynhildr was confident she could best her in a hand-to-hand fight.

Before she fully decided to launch herself at the

woman, the ground shook. The boulders protecting them from the storm rattled against the outcropping of stone, threatening to fall. Skuld stared with wide eyes as small pebbles rained down from their makeshift ceiling. "What's happening?"

Brynhildr looked just as panicked. "I don't know."

A large chunk of rock crashed down against one of the boulders that made up one of the walls of the enclosure. Brynhildr threw herself at Skuld, knocking her out of the way of the falling rocks. Gasping at the unexpected weight of Brynhildr over her, Skuld struggled. Only when the Valkyrie thought the danger of falling rocks had passed did she release Skuld from her hold.

Instead of a makeshift cave that protected them, now only two boulders remained. Their fire had been extinguished by a combination of bitter cold wind and wet whipping snow. Through the white blur of the blizzard, Skuld made out a hulking shadowy figure.

Before she could even form the words, the figure lumbered closer, the indistinct shape becoming clearer and larger than Skuld wanted. The creature towered above the Norn and the Valkyrie, limbs as thick as oaks. A stench unlike any Skuld ever encountered pierced through the freezing wind. Hair coated the creature's arms in thick, icy clumps. A knobbed club made from the trunk of a fallen tree dangled from a meaty fist. Scraggly, greasy hair lay limp atop its round and bulbous face. From what Skuld could tell in the snowbound darkness, its weathered skin appeared to be an unsettling shade of gray. Despite its hulking twenty-foot frame, the creature wore naught but haphazardly stitched together pelts across its middle. Its eyes were small and held not even a glint of what Skuld considered reason.

Clutching at Skuld and with her eyes wide, Brynhildr whispered shakily, "It's a troll! We need to run. Now!"

Chapter Four: Jǫtunheimr

Over the noise of the wind and the sleet came a deep rumble that shook Skuld to her bones. It grew louder until it ripped out of the mouth of the figure like a fierce war horn at the commencement of battle. With a mighty bellow, the troll raised its club and brought it down hard atop the fire pit, sending the dying embers scattering into the night.

"We have to go!" Brynhildr hissed as she yanked Skuld to her feet. "It will eat us if we don't get out of here now!"

Before Skuld could force her limbs to move, the club swinging troll lunged at the two women with a roar.

Deftly dodging the lumbering attack, Brynhildr unsheathed her sword and slashed at the massive gray figure as she passed by.

Skuld hesitated, unsure what to do. Strix landed on her shoulder and nipped at her ear as if to say get moving.

Infuriated by Brynhildr's attack, the troll swung his club back and forth in an attempt to smash the Valkyrie; Skuld narrowly dodged out of the way. It served as a realization that the battle with the troll was kill or be killed.

Hefting Týrfingr in her hands, she took a deep breath in and readied herself for the attack. Strix took flight, ready to fight alongside his mistress. Letting out a fierce cry, Skuld charged the troll, the sword raised and ready.

The creature, so focused on obliterating the human, wasn't prepared for Skuld's attack. The blade found purchase in the back of the troll's left calf where it sank into the thick skin a few inches before falling to the ground. The wound barely bled.

The troll reacted by batting Skuld away much like an annoying insect. Her bones cracked as she landed hard against the remaining stone wall of their makeshift shelter, knocking the wind out of her. As she lay crumpled against the stone, gasping for air, the troll turned back to Brynhildr, swiping at her.

Brynhildr attacked with a ferocity that made Skuld understand how she had become a Valkyrie at such a young age. Her fighting skill was superb; the poetry in her motions that was punctuated in the blood she spilt.

Blood dribbled out of the wounds the Valkyrie inflicted. Great rivers of dull grayish pink fluid soaked the troll's skin. Enraged, and stronger for it, the troll snatched Brynhildr up with both hands and held her high as though to smash her against the ground.

Skuld got to her feet. She couldn't let Brynhildr die. Letting out a shrill whistle that carried on the wind, she called for Strix.

From out of the darkness of the storm came the owl. With a shriek and talons extended, Strix went for the troll's beady eyes. In the wake of flapping wings, razor-sharp talons, and an equally pervasive beak, the troll staggered. He relaxed his hands and used one to swat at the offending bird, causing Brynhildr to lurch towards the ground. She gripped onto the other hand to keep from falling.

The troll's arms swung about. Brynhildr lost her grip and fell, disappearing into the blur of white. Strix kept up his attack, successfully blinding the creature.

It cried out in pain and rage, its voice drowned out from the might of the storm.

Skuld took the opportunity to rush forward again. Her sword became lost in the snow and beyond her reach, so she grabbed the hilt of her obsidian dagger. The wind whipped and she had to bring her arm up to shield her face from the stinging sleet.

With the troll's attention focused on Brynhildr, she maneuvered around to the back of the troll's legs once again.

With her dagger, she carved a bind-rune into its skin just below the scratch she made with the sword. The rune glowed, sending its power into the body of the creature. As a result, the left leg gave out causing the creature to stumble. It didn't fall. Not yet. Skuld raced to the other leg, repeating her spell.

The right leg crumpled beneath the weight of the troll. The creature collapsed onto the ground, blind, confused, and enraged.

Skuld couldn't get out from underneath the troll in time; its massive form tumbled down atop of her. She lay in the snow pinned on her side underneath the weight of its now useless right knee.

The creature bled profusely from the wounds the three had inflicted. It cried out pitifully in pain and fear. Blood wept from the creature's eye sockets, creating an even more gruesome countenance than nature gave it.

Out of the corner of her eye, she saw Brynhildr approach the troll's head from the right. The Valkyrie looked no worse for wear, though she moved slowly. She brought her sword up and stabbed it decisively into the troll's temple.

A momentary paroxysm of pain and shock rippled throughout the creature's body. One last mournful cry escaped its lips, fading into a final hiss of breath.

The knee that pinned Skuld down shifted enough so she could scurry out from under it.

"You killed it," Skuld said as she made her way to where the Valkyrie stood, picking up her discarded sword.

"Its suffering wouldn't have done anyone any good," Brynhildr responded. She knelt and wiped her sword in the snow. "It was the creature's time to die. He fought bravely."

Skuld found herself impressed by the girl's stoic demeanor in the face of taking a life. She murmured to herself, "It seems I was wrong. Perhaps you are suited for your destiny."

"What did you say?" Brynhildr asked.

Skuld shook her head. "Perhaps we should find another shelter."

"No need." Brynhildr pointed towards the brightening horizon. She stood and returned her sword to her sheath.

The long, frozen night made way for the dawn.

Beside her, the still-warm corpse of the troll crackled and shifted as the light of the sun rose higher into the clearing sky. Within moments, the heap of flesh next to her transformed into a pile of stones still wet with gray-pink blood.

"The doorway between the worlds disappeared," Skuld said as she inspected the spot where she appeared the previous day. The blizzard had passed leaving clear skies and persistent cold in its wake.

"I thought the different realms just kind of melded together." Brynhildr crossed her arms and shifted her weight to her left leg. "When I go to the battles with my sister Valkyries in Miðgarðr, we cross Bifrǫst. There are no doorways."

Skuld tried to be patient. There was so much the Valkyrie didn't understand. "Some of the realms overlap each other in certain places, but not all of them. There are also more formal and specific doorways, but those are typically hidden unless you know where to look. Not just anyone can go to those places, not even the gods."

"Do you know where the realms overlap? If we can find those places, we can make our way to Ásgarðr. Maybe one of the gods can help us get to where we belong. Or maybe I can find Óðinn and he can help us."

"The Ífingr River is the border between Ásgarðr and Jǫtunheimr. We can cross the river to get to Ásgarðr."

"Great, how far is it? Which way do we go?" Brynhildr held her arms open wide, gesturing to the barren, snow-filled landscape. "There's nothing to tell us we are going in the right direction." Her impatience made her sarcasm as sharp as a knife.

Skuld, however, remained calm. "Strix, fly ahead. See if you can locate the river. Return to me once you spot it."

The white owl hooted his affirmation into the frigid air as he leapt into flight.

"And what do we do while your pet is scouting the way? Need I remind you we killed a troll? We have to get out of here before dark, otherwise, his friends will come after us."

"Why don't you put on your swan suit and fly with Strix then? With the two of you looking, we'll find the right direction sooner."

Brynhildr's round cheeks flushed. "I can't. I told you it ripped when I saved you from the avalanche."

"Can't you mend it? You're a Valkyrie, aren't you?"

"I don't know how to fix the magic part of it. I need Óðinn or one of the other Valkyries to help me."

The Norn grunted. "That's useful."

"I didn't ask to be stranded here," Brynhildr snapped, her embarrassment turning back into anger. "I should have never pulled you out of that avalanche. Maybe if I had minded my own business, I'd have been out of here by now without the ill-luck of knowing you."

"You think I want to be trapped with you? All you do is talk and play stupid games," Skuld scoffed.

"I saved you twice last night, you wretched witch!" Irritated, Brynhildr stomped her feet in frustration. "You are such a miserable person! I ought to leave you here and make my way to Ásgarðr on my own!"

"Why don't you then?" Skuld challenged, feeling hurt. "I don't need you. If anything, you would slow me down."

All of the patience Brynhildr had for Skuld evaporated as soon as those words were uttered. In a huff, Brynhildr gathered her feathered cloak and her sword. "Goodbye, Skuld. May the gods and the giants show you no mercy." Brynhildr stomped off through the snow, abandoning the Norn to the bitter cold.

Skuld watched the Valkyrie leave, her face twisted in anger and quiet regret. "Good riddance," she muttered, trying to convince herself this was for the best. "I don't need a child clinging to me every step of the way."

As she waited for Strix to return, Skuld considered the sky above her, pale and barren of any sign of clouds. With her sisters were out of reach, she had to stick to her mission of apprehending the murderer get him back to the Well of Destiny.

Would her sisters realize she couldn't get back? Would they somehow be able to help her from their vantage points of remembrance and present? Probably not, Skuld decided.

From inside the realms, she could not shape the future. She could only do that when she carved the fates into Yggdrasil's bark. What she could see was what she was bound to. Still, despite the uncertainty of the future before her, she must press on and complete her mission.

Coming to terms with her situation, Skuld gave serious thought to what her next moves should be. To do that, she had to understand what she'd learned so far.

The weapon that killed Ratatǫskr was called Týrfingr. Dwarves created and cursed the blade. There were two of them at the present time. The one in her possession seemed to be of an impossible age. Whole creation cycles had transpired since this blade was forged. The other Týrfingr, the one from this cycle remained in possession of the dwarves, at least for the moment.

The person who wielded the blade somehow managed to survive Ragnarǫk multiple times when nothing else in the Nine Realms could. That fact spoke of someone with immense power. This person had also managed to evade detection by Skuld and her sisters for who knew how long.

The sheer lack of information about this person infuriated her. Accustomed as she was to knowing what would happen, this dearth of knowledge aggravated her to no end.

Perhaps instead of speculating on who disrupted Yggdrasil and the Nine Realms, she should be considering what the person would gain from it. Why murder Ratatǫskr? Why befoul the Well of Destiny and poison Niðhǫggr? Why run off Veðrfǫlnir? To what purpose had all of these things been done?

It must have something to do with the well. The powers of its waters were part of the magic that made the fates of all in the Nine Realms occur as well as the power behind Yggdrasil's regeneration. If anyone in the realms knew the extent of the well's powers, or even how to get to it, then there would have been scores of all manner of creatures lined up to get even the tiniest drop. The water from the well possessed the power to change the fate of anyone in the Nine Realms, with or without Skuld or her sisters.

But why destroy the well? If someone's clever enough to sneak into the home of the Nornir, why would they destroy everything? To know for sure, she had to get to the third well which fed Yggdrasil. Mímir was the guardian of the Well of Wisdom, also known as Mímisbrunnr. It contained all of the accumulated wisdom of all the Nine Realms. If her suspicions were correct, then Mímisbrunnr would be the next target for the culprit.

Strix's screech echoing in the frozen air interrupted Skuld's thoughts. The owl alighted down next to his mistress and nuzzled his head against her cheek.

"What did you see, my friend?" Skuld asked, gazing into the owl's large midnight eyes.

A flash of runes occurred in the owl's pupils and in brilliant bursts of images Skuld saw the aerial view of the landscape surrounding her. Miles and miles of desolate snow-covered rocky terrain separated her and the rushing Ífingr River which served as the gateway into the home of the Æsir gods, Ásgarðr. She stood in the heart of Jǫtunheimr and getting out would take a significant amount of time. Mímisbrunnr wasn't too far from the Ífingr River, but it was hidden by magic, something Skuld would have to deal with. But first, she had to get there.

Removing herself from the frozen rock she'd been resting on, she held her arm out for Strix. "We are off to see Mímir. He will know what we need to do."

She'd been traveling for about an hour when the ground fell out from beneath her. Her feet and legs tangled in something fine, but also incredibly strong. It wrapped around her lower extremities as she fell hard onto the cold earth several feet below the surface. Her ankle twisted painfully when she landed. As an echo of the disruption she caused, brittle twigs and dried mud debris rained down upon her. A few sharp rocks dotted the bottom of the pit she fell into, making her thankful she'd avoided hitting them on the way down.

Above her, the strange and faint chime of a bell sounded.

"What now?" Skuld muttered to herself, irritated she walked so blindly into a trap.

Strix circled in the sky above the hole Skuld found herself in. After flying over a few times, the owl flew out of sight.

Sighing, she took stock of her injuries. Besides her throbbing ankle, there were a few bumps and bruises and some aches, but otherwise, she was alright. Skuld strained against the fine spider silk mesh net around her legs. Freeing her dagger, she severed the net binding her. Tossing the scraps of netting aside, she inspected the pit. She might be able to climb out using some of the more firmly lodged rocks sticking out of the dirt.

Just as she started climbing, shadows blocked the weak sunshine and voices filtered down from the top. Over the edge of the hole, two faces peered down; both were Jǫtunn. One female and the other male.

From what Skuld could remember, Jǫtnar looked similar enough to the gods and to humans, but they were of a wilder, more visceral culture. However, even though they were cousins of the Æsir and the Vanir, the Jǫtunn practice of cannibalism set them apart. Speculation abounded that the steady diet of Jǫtnar flesh is what gave them their brutish features and their famously short tempers.

As Skuld stared into their faces, she sensed the glimmer of violence in their small set eyes.

The initial look of expectations on the Jǫtnar faces transformed to excitement at finding what appeared to be a girl stuck in their trap.

"Hello?" Skuld called, furtively reaching for the hilt of Týrfingr with her left hand.

They did not respond. Instead, the two faces disappeared, and low-pitched voices started speaking. Skuld couldn't discern what they were saying. Mentally Skuld readied herself for a fight. She refused to become some Jǫtunn's dinner.

A rope fell over the edge of the hole. The female Jǫtunn peered in at Skuld. "Come on then, let's get you out of there." She smiled, showing her mouthful of rotted teeth; an action that transformed her ugly features into flat-out hideous.

Skuld didn't like the look of hunger in the Jǫtunn's eyes or the way she licked her thin, cracked lips.

"You're going to have to come down here and get me," she answered, hefting her dagger aloft.

The female Jǫtunn's small, dark eyes narrowed at Skuld's insolence. Without saying a word, she pulled back out of sight and spoke again in low tones to her companion.

Before long, the male's head appeared at the opening of the hole. His long, scraggly blonde hair fell into his ice-blue eyes, and the wisps of hair sprouting along his cheeks gave him a scruffy appearance.

"We caught you fair and square, girl," he said in a rough voice. "You belong to us. Now get out of there. Use the rope to climb up."

Just as Skuld opened her mouth to yell back her dissent, something large struck the Jǫtunn on the side of his head. The force of the blow sent him sprawling away out from the hole. The female Jǫtunn screamed in terror. The noise reverberated through Skuld's head. She brought both of her hands to her ears in a vain attempt to block out the sound. The shriek cut off, giving way to dull, wet sounding thuds. The clink of metal clashing with metal and a few grunts followed until the cacophony died off into an uneasy silence.

Skuld craned her neck, trying to see what happened beyond the viewpoint of the sky directly above the hole. It was no use. She could only see the pale blue of the sky.

Skuld didn't like the silence. She shifted her weight back and forth between her feet, noticing the ache from her twisted ankle. She held her dagger at the ready.

Snow tumbled over the edge of the trap and the noise of shuffling feet through the slush made her adjust the dagger. Should a Jǫtunn poke their head over into her line of sight, she would let the dagger fly.

The face that did appear wasn't one Skuld ever thought she'd see again. Brynhildr smiled down at her from the top of the trap and the Norn had to forcibly stop herself from throwing the dagger.

"Well look what we have here! Caught yourself in a food trap, did you?" the smugness in Brynhildr's tone grated on Skuld's nerves. Perhaps she should have thrown the dagger.

"What are you doing here?" Skuld demanded. "I thought you were off to Ásgarðr?"

"And leave you behind helpless? I wouldn't dream of it. You'd never survive on your own without me to save you all the time," Brynhildr tittered. "You are safe now, so come on out of the trap."

Furious about being saved by a slip of a human girl for the third time in the space of a day, Skuld climbed her way out of the trap, doing her best not to aggravate her swelling ankle. When she reached the top of the hole, strong arms that certainly didn't belong to Brynhildr hoisted her out the rest of the way.

Startled, Skuld found herself face to face with none other than Þórr. The Æsir God of Thunder gave her a warm smile, the corners of his blue eyes crinkling as the edges of his auburn beard drew upwards. Behind the god sat a large chariot hitched to a pair of white goats with horns budding atop their heads.

"You weren't wrong, little sister," Þórr said, his voice deep and booming. "She does appear very strange indeed."

"Put me down at once, Þórr. Or you shall regret it," Skuld growled. She scowled until he laughingly obliged.

"Such an ungrateful little beast, isn't she?" Þórr said to Brynhildr.

"She is, but she's helpless," the Valkyrie mused.

"She would appreciate it if you didn't talk about her as though she will not be here," Skuld spat. "Furthermore, she will not need help."

Brynhildr laughed. "Sure you don't. You were just going to be eaten by Jǫtnar. If Þórr and I hadn't found you, you would be on their campfire spit right about now."

Skuld didn't have an answer, so she leveled her gaze on the white owl perched on a nearby branch. "Traitor," she snarled. "You went to find her, didn't you?"

Strix preened his feathers nonchalantly.

"Your pet got you help," Brynhildr interjected. "You should be thanking him."

Þórr shook his mane of red hair and slung his hammer over his shoulder, not at all concerned with the squabbling of the young Valkyrie and her strange friend. "Well, little sister. Now that we've found your prickly friend, I must be off. Jǫrmungandr awaits me as Father awaits you. And you know as well as I that Father does not have patience for excuses." With that warning, Þórr made his way to his chariot.

Brynhildr ran after the god, "Wait Þórr! Please take us to Ásgarðr. I cannot fly and if we tried to walk, we would never get there in time."

Þórr frowned at her. "But I am going to fish for Jǫrmungandr, the world serpent. I do not have time to take you to Father."

"Please, Þórr?"

The God of Thunder relented. "Alright, but we must hurry. I think I can catch the great serpent this time."

Elated, the Valkyrie turned her attention back to Skuld. "Are you coming with us to Ásgarðr, or would you like to wait around for more Jǫtnar who would love to have you for lunch?"

Skuld glowered at Brynhildr. "I'm not going to Ásgarðr. There is a better way for me to find the one I am looking for."

"Oh, do tell!" Brynhildr gushed sarcastically. "I can't wait to hear what you've come up with! Who else besides the Æsir could possibly help you with your quest?"

She regarded the Valkyrie coldly. "I am going to visit Mímir the Wise. If anyone in the Nine Realms can help guide me, he can."

Her answer stunned Brynhildr for a moment. "What do you mean you are going to see Mímir the Wise? He's nothing more than a legend. A character in a story long ago told."

"Come, Bryn!" Þórr called from his chariot. "We must go."

"Wait a moment!" Brynhildr shouted. To Skuld she said, "Mímisbrunnr doesn't exist."

Skuld shrugged. "What you think doesn't matter. This is not your quest. I know Mímir is real and I know Mímisbrunnr is just beyond the Ífingr River." The Norn brushed off her cloak and made sure the old sword Týrfingr was securely fastened to her belt. She began walking, sure Brynhildr would not follow. It would be better if she didn't; Skuld did not want to risk the Valkyrie's fate.

"Wait a minute!" the Valkyrie ran after her. "You can't be serious."

"How can a human Valkyrie who has witnessed so many improbable things have such little faith that a single wise person exists? Really, Brynhildr."

Brynhildr made a face at Skuld's condescension. "I know what you are trying to do. You can't get rid of me that easily. You wouldn't survive. I left you alone for what, a couple of hours and then what happened? You were about to be lunch for some hungry Jǫtnar. Face it, Skuld. You need me."

Skuld sniffed and refused to look at the Valkyrie, however the point the young human made hit home.

Sensing that she was listening, Brynhildr made a compromising plea. "At least travel with Þórr and I to the Ífingr River. It will be quicker than you walking there, especially with a twisted ankle."

Skuld considered the offer. The young Valkyrie was right; traveling via chariot would be much faster than walking. It would give her time to heal her ankle. Plus, traveling with Þórr through Jǫtunheimr would be much safer than alone; he had a fearsome reputation of being a Jǫtunn-killer.

"Alright fine," she conceded at last. "I will let you travel with me as far as the Ífingr River."

Again, the Valkyrie's light, silvery laugh rang out through the icy air. "Oh, Skuld. You're going to make me regret this, aren't you?"

Skuld grit her teeth. The journey would be long indeed.

Together the two made their way back to where Þórr waited in the chariot, Brynhildr purposefully slowing her stride to match Skuld's limping gait.

"Ready?" he asked as they climbed into the chariot with him.

Brynhildr answered for both of them. "Yes, we are. To the River Ífingr!"

The God of Thunder gave her a sidelong glance at the destination but said nothing. He snapped the reins, sending the goats forward. Skuld whistled and Strix soared after them, keeping pace.

The desolate landscape of Jǫtunheimr morphed as the trio progressed along their journey. From nothing but rocks and ice came sporadic, hardy evergreen shrubs which grew taller and taller until they became larger and larger trees. At last, they found themselves in a thick snow-covered forest. Evergreens gave a respite of color in the stark white and gray of deep winter.

Brynhildr made it her mission to talk nonstop during the entire journey. Or at least that's how it seemed to Skuld. No matter how much she begged for silence, the Valkyrie just kept jabbering about the inanest topics. Þórr joined in, happy for the conversation in a normally dull journey.

In a matter of hours, Skuld knew so much more about the youngest Valkyrie to ever ride alongside Óðinn and his hot-tempered son than she wanted. Even when she thought all of the topics in the Nine Realms were exhausted, the girl and the god still found more to say.

They had traveled for quite some time when the conversation began to lull. Skuld brightened at the prolonged silences where she could think. She used the time bouncing in the strange contraption Þórr guided through the landscape to heal her ankle.

"Skuld here says she's a Norn," Brynhildr told Þórr after a minute or two of silence.

"A Norn?" Þórr repeated, sounding impressed. "What are you doing away from the Well of Destiny?" He glanced back at Skuld who pointedly refused to look at either of her companions.

"You believe her?" Brynhildr questioned. "She doesn't seem very Norn-like."

Þórr laughed. "And you don't seem very Valkyrie-like. You should not judge people so."

Brynhildr considered what he said while staring speculatively at Skuld. "I guess I just thought Nornir would be more, I dunno. Regal or something."

"I apologize for not living up to your mighty expectations," Skuld replied. She kept her gaze out to the passing landscape.

Brynhildr cast a pointed look at Þórr. "What if she's lying?"

The God of Thunder shrugged. "What if she's not? A Norn is a very powerful being. They can end your life on a whim and erase you completely from the Nine Realms. Are you willing to anger one as powerful as that? Remember, it costs nothing to take a person by their word until it is proven otherwise. If their word is false, it is they who are shamed."

The girl bit her lip.

Þórr twisted to look at Skuld. "I've always been curious. What is it that Nornir do? I mean, besides carve all of our fates into the great tree."

Skuld hesitated in answering. Once she participated

in their conversation, then more and more questions would come.

"See?" Brynhildr piped up. "She cannot answer. I don't think she's being honest."

Those words set Skuld's blood pumping. "My sisters and I care for Yggdrasil. We coat its roots in the mud from the Well of Destiny and we carve the fates of the Nine Realms into Yggdrasil's bark to make sure the seasons are followed. We ensure the people of the Nine Realms adhere to their fates, thereby guaranteeing the proper chain of events."

Brynhildr crossed her arms over her chest. "It still seems to be an impossible task for just three of you."

"Why do the logistics of it matter when you don't believe I am a Norn in the first place?" Skuld retorted.

"I just think there are many more probable things in this world other than an omniscient being who is stuck in the Nine Realms and can't get home."

"I never claimed to be omniscient. You twist my words, Valkyrie."

"Woah," Þórr said and drew his goats to a halt. "We have reached the Ífingr River."

Once the squeaking wooden chariot rolled to a halt, Skuld heard the dull roar of the fast-moving river echoed off of the trees. Just ahead a small overhang of rock looked out over the riverbank below.

Skuld jumped out of the chariot and went to peer over the cliff's edge at the flowing water two dozen feet down. It was a wide river, the opposite bank a mile away from their vantage point. On the other side lay the outskirts of Ásgarðr, land of the gods.

With bitter winter winds whistling through the bare trees of Jǫtunheimr, those same winds transformed to chill autumn breezes rustling through crisp and brittle leaves in Ásgarðr. The other side of the river was awash in reds, golds, browns, and yellows. The sun seemed to shine softer. The land of the Æsir felt more inviting and less primal than where they stood in Jǫtunheimr.

The seasons were off, Skuld thought. It shouldn't be the dead of winter in Jǫtunheimr and then autumn in Ásgarðr. Had time shifted between all of the realms? Yggdrasil's health must be tenuous indeed to make time slip in such a way.

"How are we going to cross that?" Brynhildr breathed as she came up behind Skuld. Her tone gave away how much the fast-rushing water intimidated her. "We need a boat or something. It's too dangerous to swim across."

"We?" Skuld asked, giving her a sidelong glance. The Valkyrie fixed her anxious gaze at the river, her brows furrowed as though if she concentrated enough the water wouldn't reach up and drown her.

"I need not cross the river. Mímisbrunnr is north of here and still in Jǫtunheimr."

"Here is where I leave you," Þórr announced from the chariot. He waved his hammer above him. "There is a world serpent to catch and many miles between me and him."

Brynhildr backed away from the edge of the overhang and returned to the chariot. Instead of getting on along with Þórr, she grabbed her feathered cloak and gave the mighty God of Thunder a warm embrace.

"Safe travels, Þórr," she said.

"And to you, little sister." He glanced over to where Skuld watched the exchange in confused horror. "Watch yourself."

With a loud click and a snap of the reins, Þórr's goats wheeled around and ran back the way they came. The God of Thunder waved once before disappearing around the bend, leaving the Norn and the Valkyrie behind.

"I thought you and he were going to Ásgarðr?" Skuld demanded when the Valkyrie trudged back to her.

Brynhildr shrugged. "I've never been to one of the three wells before. This is an adventure I cannot miss."

She glanced back over f at the raging river. "Besides, you said Mímisbrunnr is in Jǫtunheimr, so we don't have to cross the river?"

"Yes," Skuld responded, still not quite sure what was happening.

"Good," Brynhildr sighed. "I don't know how to swim. Which way to Mímisbrunnr?"

Still caught off guard by the girl's tenacity and not sure what else to do to dissuade her from tagging along, Skuld pointed to a path following the ridgeline. "This way."

The two began their trek in silence. While not on the narrow riverbank itself, they could still hear the rushing water.

Grateful for the distance from the water, Brynhildr followed Skuld's lead, though it wasn't long when she questioned the decision. "How do you know we're going the right way? No one has ever seen Mímir or his well."

Skuld took in a deep breath of cold air, filling her lungs and extending her senses. The exposed root of Yggdrasil and the power of the well that nourished it felt like a heartbeat in her mind, throbbing in the distance. The sensation, both familiar and foreign, hit Skuld with an odd sense of nostalgia. The sudden wave of homesickness made her words come out clipped and her tone didn't invite any more conversation. "I just know."

For the first time since Skuld met her, Brynhildr became quiet, even contemplative. They walked in silence, allowing the roar of the river to set their pace.

An urgent screech from Strix broke the relative peace. The owl had flown ahead, hunting for unwary mice. The announcement of his return indicated something unexpected ahead. The owl landed in his customary spot on the Norn's shoulder. His earsplitting screeches turned to low toned hoots and coos.

In response, Skuld locked eyes with Strix to see what he had seen. When her vision returned to her, she stroked the downy feathers on Strix's head and turned to Brynhildr. "There's another traveler up ahead. If we keep our current pace, we will catch up to them in the next few miles."

The news made Brynhildr smile. "Let's go then."

"Wait!" Skuld called, sudden concern washing through her. "Shouldn't we be more careful? We don't know what the traveler is. Strix only saw it from above. What if it's another Jǫtunn? Or a troll? Or worse?"

"Troll's don't come out in the day time," Brynhildr replied, turning to give Skuld an exasperated sigh. "What does the traveler look like according to your bird?"

"From what Strix saw, the stranger is old and wears a large, brimmed hat."

"There! You see? Nothing to be frightened of unless you are against old people or hats."

"But it doesn't mean it's not a Jǫtunn," Skuld argued.

"We'll be careful. If we are going to make it to Mímisbrunnr, then we have to keep going. Are you going to let your fear of a few Jǫtnar stop you from your quest?"

The Valkyrie's words made sense, though Skuld didn't want to admit it. Her close call with the cannibalistic Jǫtnar had shaken her more than she thought. Muttering under her breath, Skuld walked with Brynhildr along the path.

Chapter Five: Mímisbrunnr

Before long Skuld and Brynhildr saw the makings of a camp in the middle of a small clearing. As the sun began to set, the two women hesitated at the edge of the tree line as they decided what to do.

The old man called out in a strong, commanding voice from his position at the fire, "It's going to get very cold soon. Better to reveal yourselves now and come warm yourselves by the fire instead of freezing to death in the forest."

Both Brynhildr and Skuld gasped in recognition. Brynhildr got up from their hiding spot and ran towards the old man and the promise of warmth.

Skuld followed at a slower pace, watching as the Valkyrie advanced towards the old man. He heard her coming. With a great exhalation of breath, he rose to his feet and turned to watch them approach, his hands folded expectant in front of him.

"Brynhildr," he greeted her. "I didn't think I'd find you here." There was no hint of surprise in his tone.

The Valkyrie dipped her head in a quick bow as she responded, "All-Father. I am surprised to see you too. What brings you to Jǫtunheimr?"

"My business is my own, foster-daughter. However, I am interested to know why you are roaming the Jǫtunheimr wilderness instead of reporting to Valhǫll where you are expected."

Brynhildr's shoulders slumped at the rebuke. "I got caught in a storm and damaged my swan skin. I've been helping a woman just as lost as I make her way to Mímisbrunnr."

The man frowned and looked to where Skuld stopped, his large, weathered hand ran over his gray beard in thought.

Brynhildr, oblivious to the undercurrent of recognition between the god and her companion, endeavored to make introductions. "Skuld, I want you to meet Óðinn. Óðinn, this is Skuld."

"I know who he is," the Norn stated flatly. She pinned the old man in place with her fierce gaze and tilted her head to the side. "We've not yet met in this cycle. You've yet to make your sacrifice."

The image of Óðinn hanging by his neck from one of the branches of Yggdrasil flashed across her mind. Oh, how he suffered when he sacrificed himself. She had watched him struggle as she carved the next to his twitching and convulsing body. It seemed foolish to her but then again, she wasn't in Óðinn's position. It could very well be worth the days of agony for the glimpse of the runes and what their power could mean to one from the realms.

Óðinn regarded Skuld impassively, his bearded mouth set in a grim line. If the oddness of the young woman's words affected him, he didn't show it. "And I recognize you, Norn. You and your sisters hold much power over the realms."

"It's true then?" Brynhildr interjected. "She's really one of the Nornir?"

Óðinn gave a solemn nod of his head. "That she is. And, if I am not mistaken, she is the one who holds dominion over what ought to be."

Skuld pressed her lips into a thin line. "That's not quite how it works, but I suppose it's an accurate enough description. My sister Urðr sees the past and my sister

Verðandi the present."

Brynhildr's eyes widened and she gazed at Skuld as though she'd never before seen her. The regard in which she held the strange woman shifted. The familiarity and the comfort the young Valkyrie expressed so early on in their hesitant acquaintance vanished, replaced with fear.

The change made Skuld uncomfortable. Even as annoying as the Valkyrie could be, she hadn't wanted Brynhildr to fear her.

"It has been a long time since you and your sisters have walked the realms," Óðinn admitted, shifting his stance. He tried to hide his unease, but Skuld saw right through the façade. "Tell me, Norn, what beckons you from your duties for the tree? What dire importance pulled you away from carving the fate of the worlds?"

"I am looking for someone," Skuld said, preferring to keep her answer short and to the point. Óðinn gobbled up knowledge like a starving man. If he were to know the calamitous significance of her mission, how would he use and twist that knowledge for his own gain? She feared it would be in ways that would further disrupt the fine balance of time's progression.

Óðinn mused, "I dare say someone must be mighty to evade your sight, Norn. Is this why you seek Mímir the Wise?"

Eager to end this particular conversation, Skuld focused on the old god's motives instead. She brought her hand up and drew invisible runes in the air between her and the old god. They allowed her to see his path and where it led. The haziness was less with him than it had been with Brynhildr. The future was more certain with Óðinn. When she finished, she blinked away the sight.

"You are heading to Mímisbrunnr, aren't you? You intend to barter your eye for a drink from Mímir's Well."

The glower that came over the god's face intended to instill terror.

Despite the threatening look, Skuld persisted. "You

should know while you will gain a great amount of wisdom, it will not be the knowledge you seek."

"You don't know that," Óðinn snapped in a rare show of temper.

Arching an eyebrow, Skuld asked, "Don't I, One Eye?"

A cold silence descended over the group, only broken by the occasional crackle of the fire. Eager to dispel the tension in the air, Brynhildr piped up with a question. "How far are we from Mímisbrunnr, All-Father?"

Forcing his scowling gaze away from Skuld, Óðinn answered, "Not far. Once dawn breaks, it will take us until midday to reach the well." After a long moment of consideration, Óðinn gestured to his camp and offered a formal welcome. "While this is not my home or my hearth, warm your bones near the fire. If you are hungry, have some of the fish I caught in the river. Please, sit and find rest."

"Thank you," Skuld bowed her head graciously. The warmth was delicious to her freezing limbs and she held her hands out to the flames, thankful for the heat. It didn't cease to astonish her how extreme weather could get inside the Nine Realms. Her home among the branches of Yggdrasil was temperate and even.

As both of the women settled at the fire, Óðinn turned his back on them and whispered a couple of incantations. The air around the camp shimmered. Skuld felt the power of a protection spell encircle them. Having set the protective barrier, Óðinn returned to the campfire.

Brynhildr sat between Skuld and Óðinn, quiet and contemplative for once. As Óðinn began preparing the fish, the young Valkyrie found her voice once again. This time her questions were directed at the god. A fact which made Skuld grateful. She listened as she released Strix to hunt for the evening, watching him fly far above the old god's magic.

"All-Father, what is the news from Ásgarðr? Is it true we are going to war?"

Óðinn deftly scaled the four fish and skewered them on thin twigs he'd trimmed earlier. As he finished each one, he handed the twigs to Brynhildr who situated them above the fire. "Yes, war is looming. The Vanir sent a witch called Gullveig into our midst to confound us and catch us unawares. A provocation on their end which inevitably would bring about war. Each side is gathering their forces. The battle will commence soon. Which is why I summoned the Valkyries to Valhǫll."

Brynhildr bit her lip and nodded, thinking through the implications of a war between two tribes of gods. "I don't know much about how the Vanir fight. What are their weaknesses?"

Óðinn couldn't mask the pride in his eyes. "That's the Brynhildr I know. Always looking for the advantage." He shifted his gaze to Skuld. "But this must be boring for you, Skuld. Battle plans and strategies for an outcome you already know."

Skuld knew better than to fall into that trap. The old god fished for information to aid his cause. "On the contrary," she said. "I rarely get the chance to understand events from a mortal perspective. Please, continue. I will not interrupt."

While unhappy at not gaining a battle edge from the Norn, Óðinn gave a gracious smile and inclined his head. Wise men and gods dare not challenge one of the Nornir. Óðinn wasn't fool enough to make an enemy of her while she walked the Nine Realms.

The All-Father gave the skewered fish a couple of pokes to make sure they were fully cooked. As he offered each of the women their shares, he said, "Very well. Brynhildr, I will tell you about the Vanir as we eat."

Skuld accepted her meal and settled in to listen to what Óðinn had to say. This proved to be a once in a lifetime chance to understand from a mortal's perspective how the things she carved came to be.

When all of the food had been served, Óðinn explained, "While the Vanir are also gods, it's important to understand that they are vastly different from the Æsir. Their practices are not . . ." Óðinn struggled to find the right words. "Their ideas about the world are wrong."

"What do you mean wrong?" Brynhildr asked between bites of fish.

"They perform perverse magical arts to gain unholy power. They shirk away from fair and honest hand to hand combat. Instead, they favor trickery and cunning. The Vanir are untrustworthy and will cheat you out of your last coin given half a chance. They have no moral compass; their actions are controlled by whims and passing fancies. But they are crafty, and you will want to believe the insincere words they speak. I warn you; it would be the last mistake you ever make if you do listen to them."

"What sort of magic do they have?" Brynhildr asked, soaking up the knowledge eagerly. "Battle magic?"

To keep from making faces at Óðinn's biased descriptions, Skuld settled back and closed her eyes with her belly full of fish. She listened with skepticism to the ensuing tales of treachery and inaccurate portrayals of what she knew to be a tribe of gods very similar to the Æsir.

After a while, when Óðinn had recited his full litany of propaganda, Skuld heard her name whispered in their hushed tones. Keeping her eyes closed, she focused on the sound of their voices to understand what they were saying.

Brynhildr's became the first distinct voice. "She's not as powerful as you think. I've saved her life three times since yesterday. If she is as powerful as you say, then something has happened for her to lose her edge."

"Stupid girl, think! The problem isn't her power. She shouldn't be here at all. This is a dangerous precedence.

It means the Nornir are interfering with what has already been written on Yggdrasil. Something they cannot change from there. Something is very wrong."

"Then we leave her to her business, and we get on with ours. After we visit Mímir the Wise, I will go with you back to Valhǫll to prepare for the coming war."

"No, it's too risky to allow her to roam about unattended. We need to keep her on our side. It is bad luck to cross a Norn, but it would be much worse if the Vanir won her over. We would lose everything. I will not allow that to happen."

"So do we keep her with us?"

"Not with us. You will stay with her. Travel with her and make sure she completes whatever mission she is here to do. Protect her. Make sure she does not fall into the hands of the Vanir."

"But the coming war," Brynhildr protested. "What about my duty as a Valkyrie?"

"Your duty is to obey me," Óðinn countered. "Your time to fight will come, young one. For now, you are meant for more important things. Do not give her a reason to side with the Vanir or the war will already be lost."

A heavy sigh escaped the young Valkyrie's lips. "Alright then."

"Good girl. Now, get some rest. Dawn will be here soon."

Skuld remained silent, considering what she'd heard. The All-Father counted her as an asset for the coming war. It meant she would be stuck with Brynhildr for the time being. While the prospect did not thrill her, Óðinn wouldn't allow her to leave his sight unless Brynhildr journeyed with her.

What's more, Óðinn didn't know about the befouling of the Well of Destiny. Skuld vowed to keep it that way. If the god knew of the danger to Yggdrasil, he would use that knowledge to bend the cycle to change the outcome of Ragnarǫk to his favor. He was arrogant enough to think he could change fate when it suited him. If that happened, everything would crumble. Yggdrasil would hasten to its death and there would be naught Skuld or her sisters could do.

Óðinn was and will be a major force in the Nine Realms. Where he walked, so went destiny. If she couldn't get back to her home to undo whatever changes he made, how could she keep the All-Father on the right path and keep Ragnarǫk on track?

Dawn came with clear skies. Óðinn dozed by the embers of the night's fire, snoring into his chest. Brynhildr huddled under her travel cloak on the ground, her mouth open with drool freezing on her lips and chin.

Skuld sat up and stretched in the cold morning air. Her back was stiff from the hard ground and her muscles ached with the unaccustomed use. She missed her solid hut and comfortable bed.

After allowing herself the moment of pity, Skuld rose to her feet and approached the edge of camp where Óðinn's protection spell still shimmered in the air. The casting was rough and haphazard, but it was strong, realm-based magic originating from Miðgarðr. With a few twists of her fingers to shape the bind-rune and her whispered intention, Skuld opened a pathway through the protection spell so she could venture back into the woods to relieve herself.

The woods were quiet in the dawn; not even birds broke the serenity of the trees. Skuld completed her business and made her way back to camp.

Along the way, the familiar rush of feathered wings and a low-pitched screech heralded Strix's landing on Skuld's shoulder.

"Hello, Strix," Skuld said and rubbed her fingers under the owl's chin. "Did you hunt well last night, friend?"

The owl hooted in response. Skuld smiled and

together they re-entered the camp. Both Óðinn and Brynhildr were awake; Óðinn tended to the fire, dousing the fading embers with snow. The ice hissed as it hit the smoldering ashes and the resulting steam rose into the air.

Brynhildr wiped the sleep from her eyes and stretched. When she saw Skuld, she smiled. "Good morning! Did you sleep well?"

Either she'd gotten used to the idea of what Skuld was or she pretended. The Norn couldn't tell which. Sensing Óðinn's gray eyes watching her, Skuld remembered she too had a part to play.

"Yes," she said and forced her lips into a smile.

"You got past my barrier," Óðinn noted. "Impressive."

Skuld shrugged, not thinking before she spoke. "You have much power but have yet to gain the power of the runes."

The ugly red flush of anger tinged Óðinn's face. The insult she'd delivered was unintentional, but now impossible to retract.

However, Óðinn knew he could not afford to be tricked into reactionary anger. Gruffly, he said, "Come on then. Gather your things. Mímisbrunnr awaits."

As the trio trudged through the woods and the closer they got to Mímisbrunnr, the more intensely Skuld felt the power of the well. The distant heartbeat that echoed hers got steadier and louder with every step. Never before did she feel the power of the wells like this. Almost as if it cried out in pain and helplessness. Had the murderer been to this third well too? Had Mímisbrunnr been poisoned? Skuld couldn't voice these thoughts aloud, though the worry ate her up inside.

"Are you alright?" Brynhildr whispered as she fell in stride beside Skuld. "You don't look so good."

"I'm fine," Skuld replied. The distracting echo throughout her body made it difficult for her words to come out correctly. "I can feel the well. We are almost there."

"That's right," Óðinn confirmed coming up behind the two women. "Mímisbrunnr is just beyond those trees." He pointed a few dozen feet ahead to where a thick grove of yew trees clustered around a small clearing. The faint hint of black smoke smudged the sky above the treetops and an acrid wind brought the stench of burning.

"Something isn't right," Skuld said more to herself, but both Óðinn and Brynhildr heard the horror in her voice. Without thinking, Skuld took off running towards the grove of trees, Strix taking flight after her.

"Skuld! Wait!" Brynhildr cried out from behind her. The Valkyrie gave a helpless look to Óðinn before sprinting off after her charge.

The muscles in Skuld's legs seized as she ran. Her lungs, fueled by the freezing winter air, caught fire as she pressed forward. Despite the pain, she fought through the grove of trees, not even noticing the scratches the bare limbs left on her skin. Her progress stalled as she hit the magical barrier encircling Mímisbrunnr.

The rune spell which created this protection was a thousand times stronger than the Miðgarðr magic Óðinn used to protect the camp. Hissing in frustration, Skuld pulled out the obsidian dagger and started attacking the barrier, scratching the runes to undo its magic with both haste and force. It took multiple tries to get the magical locks undone, but it happened.

When Skuld broke through to the clearing, she came to a halt brought up short by what awaited her.

Mímir's small home, so similar to the hut she and her sisters shared, had been destroyed. Broken pieces of timber were scattered about, splintered bits of furniture and torn fabric soaked up the wet snow and froze in the wind. The home had been set on fire. As the Norn stared in horror at the remains, she noted the fire was mostly out, reducing the structure to a faded blackened husk of burning embers.

Mímir himself lay prone in the middle of the clearing, blood seeping out of a deep wound in his stomach. Next to him rested his long sword, the tip darkened by blood.

Skuld rushed to Mímir. He barely breathed, but he still lived. Cradling his head in her lap, she whispered, "What has become of you?"

The wisest of all the gods cried out in pain. "Norn," he gasped, recognizing her.

"What happened? Who did this to you?"

Brynhildr arrived in the clearing and sucked in a surprised gasp as she saw the destruction. Seeing Skuld and Mímir, she ran over to see if she could help.

"That stomach wound isn't good," she said after giving Mímir a once over glance.

"I know!" Skuld snapped. Turning back to Mímir, she asked, "Who did this?"

Mímir struggled for words. His gray hair fell in haphazard curls, giving his weathered and wrinkled face, a halo of sorts. His wizened blue eyes filled with pain. His mouth opened and closed as though he were a fish gasping for air. At last, he choked out the word "Vanaheimr."

Skuld seized that bit of information. "Vanaheimr? Do you mean to tell me one of the Vanir did this?" She pressed her shaking hands to his wound, tracing healing runes along the edges of his flesh.

The runes sealed the wound, but the damage had already been done.

Mímir shook his head in a violent shudder. "Vanaheimr magic. Rune-less fate."

"Stop speaking in riddles!" Skuld shouted, frustrated beyond measure. "Tell me plainly. I need to stop this before Yggdrasil dies! Tell me!" She gave Mímir a shake to get him to focus.

"Hey!" Brynhildr reached out and halted Skuld from doing more damage to the dying god. "Stop. You're causing him more pain. It's making things worse."

The Norn snarled at the Valkyrie, but the young woman stood her ground. Familiar with fatal wounds, Brynhildr reached into a small pouch attached to her belt and withdrew a few green leaves. She pressed the leaves into Mímir's mouth. "Here. This should ease the pain."

Mímir didn't even chew what Brynhildr gave him, choosing instead to spit them out whole so he could issue one final warning to Skuld. "Vanaheimr."

His body shuddered and convulsed and he let out one last anguished cry. By the time the sound faded from his lips, Mímir fell motionless. His wise blue eyes were no longer clouded with pain, but there no spark remained in them either. The wisest of all the gods died in Skuld's lap.

Óðinn came through the yew grove just as Skuld gingerly placed Mímir's head onto the ground.

"What happened?" the All-Father demanded. He strode over to Mímir the Wise's body and knelt as though not believing his eyes.

Shaken by the senseless destruction and the mystery of Mímir's final words, Skuld backed away from the corpse. She strayed to the well, wondering what horrors she would find in its depths.

The Well of Wisdom remained clean and pure. No hint of desecration or contamination could be found.

Óðinn spoke, his voice breaking her out of her astonishment, "Looks like I won't need to lose my eye after all. With Mímir dead, I can drink my fill for free." Óðinn approached Skuld and the well.

The words shocked Skuld back to the matter at hand. No, this wasn't right. This wasn't how things were supposed to go. Óðinn *had* to lose his eye. That was one of the fixed, definitive points in the cycle. She had to do something.

As Óðinn closed the distance between them, Skuld

made her decision. Relying on her gut instinct and her knowledge in needed to transpire to keep the cycle of Yggdrasil on track, Skuld drew Týrfingr and turned to square off against Óðinn.

The sight of the Norn with a weapon drawn brought Óðinn up short. "What is the meaning of this?"

"You will not drink from the Well of Wisdom without paying the price," Skuld said gravely.

Óðinn laughed with false bravado as he sized up his opponent. He did not expect this level of fierceness or passion from one so aloof. Still, her power to erase him from the realms made him careful. It would be unwise to underestimate her.

"Why shouldn't I drink?" he asked, keeping the smile and easy-going stance in the face of her threatening posture. "That is what I came here to do."

Skuld kept herself planted between him and Mímir's well. "If you wish to drink of the Well of Wisdom, then the price must be paid. Give me your eye."

"Why would I do that? The guardian of this well is dead, that means the water is free for the taking." Óðinn crossed his arms in front of him, his easy smile disappearing in an instant. "You would deny me the wisdom I seek?"

Skuld shook her head but kept Týrfingr at the ready. "I deny you nothing. I only ask you to pay the price as you have done countless cycles before. All that has changed is that I am the one asking, not Mímir the Wise. While I am not the guardian for the Well of Wisdom, I am still a guardian."

Óðinn weighed his options, calculating his chance of victory without self-mutilation. She was a slip of a girl, this Norn of what should be. And what battle experience would she have being sequestered in the branches of Yggdrasil? He decided he could overpower her easily.

Óðinn advanced, a confident step which caused Skuld to swipe at the air with the sword.

"You refuse to pay the price?" Skuld asked, arching an eye an eyebrow at the audacity of the god.

"I'll not give you my eye," Óðinn answered. "Move out of my way."

Skuld shifted her stance, ready to fight. "Alright. Then I will take what is owed before you drink." She leapt at Óðinn, bringing Týrfingr high over her head with the intent of bringing it down as hard as she could upon the god.

Óðinn dodged, missing the Norn's attack. With a swift movement, he reached out, grabbed hold of the sword, and yanked it out of her hands. He tossed it to the other end of the clearing. He then grasped Skuld by the front of her tunic and shoved her backward towards where Brynhildr sat with Mímir's body.

Skuld landed hard, but got back up. Frustration and fury fueled Skuld's determination to stop the god. Unable to match him physically meant she would have to best him with magic. She just had to get close enough.

With a growl, she launched herself back at the god.

"Stop it!" Brynhildr shouted, tackling Skuld to the ground.

"Let me go!" shrieked Skuld. She kicked the Valkyrie away from her and scrambled back to her feet. "He can't drink the water!"

To keep the Valkyrie away, she drew a small barrier between them, her runes scribbled into the dirt. By the way the barricade wavered in the air, Skuld knew it wasn't going to last long. She just hoped it would give her enough time to stop Óðinn without Brynhildr interfering.

Skuld picked up a half-burnt and splintered piece of wood. As she charged towards the smirking god, she carved a spell with her dagger. When she came near enough, she threw the piece of wood towards Óðinn. In mid-flight, the wood exploded, sending sharpened splinters towards the old god.

Óðinn held up his staff and chanted furiously. A glow

emanated from the staff, shielding him from most of the missiles. A few grazed his arm, ripping through the thick woven fabric of his tunic.

With more confidence, Óðinn spoke another charm to freeze her in place. The incantation he uttered bound her tight with invisible ropes. He would deal with her once he had his fill from the well. Believing he rendered the furious Norn helpless, Óðinn turned his back on her and went for his prize.

On his way, he kicked a cracked, ash-covered drinking horn with his foot. The All-Father picked it up and wiped at the dirt and ash with his robe.

Enraged, Skuld silently undid the spell Óðinn so foolishly placed upon her. When she broke free, she took up her obsidian dagger once again.

Before she made even a step in his direction, Óðinn held out a hand behind him and clenched his fist. As a result, her breath became trapped in her throat. Her lungs compressed as if they were about to implode.

Skuld struggled against the foreign magic feebly. Every movement she made caused the invisible grip on her lungs to grow tighter.

She collapsed to the ground, unable to fight. She drew in shaking, shallow breaths and forced herself to lay still. She refused to die like this, at the hands of Óðinn. She had to outsmart him. The incantation he used was vicious, but not without its weaknesses. It still connected to Óðinn. If she concentrated, she could use the runes to sever the connection. With any luck, she could strip him of this power as well. Her mastery of the runes could easily undo this spell.

Óðinn allowed himself a smug smile believing he just killed a Norn; something none of the other gods could boast. Soon, he would have all of the knowledge of the realms with just a mere drink of the Well of Wisdom. Victory over the Vanir would be next. After that, well, time would tell.

He turned his back on the dying Norn and strode towards the Well of Wisdom, eager for his hard-won prize.

No whispered incantation preceded her attack. The only thing that alerted Óðinn to Skuld's running advancement was Brynhildr's shout from behind the Norn's barricade.

"Father, watch out!"

The All-Father turned in time for Skuld to leap onto him, knocking them both to the ground. Faster than he could blink, Skuld straddled his chest traced a bind-rune under his flowing beard to pin him to the ground.

The old god drew in a sharp, rasping breath of surprise and pain.

Brynhildr pounded against the magical barrier as she cried out in anger, "Stop! Skuld, what are you doing?"

Skuld knew she didn't have much time before the hastily erected barricade crumbled and Brynhildr swept into the fray. This was her one chance. With quick, decisive movements, Skuld brought her obsidian dagger down onto Óðinn's face, removing his left eye from its socket.

Blood gushed and Óðinn cried out in pain. His screams reminded Skuld of the last time he hung himself from the branches of Yggdrasil. The cries of the god as he swung for nine long nights haunted her long after he left. Now she held the soft, jellied orb of his eyeball in her hand, listening to his agony all over again.

Swiftly she removed herself from above the bleeding god and placed her prize into a small woven pouch attached to her belt. With a wave of her fingers, she released the binding runes.

Óðinn's hands flew to his face, wiping away the blood. He sat up and screamed, this time not from pain, but rage.

"You took my eye!" He bellowed at the Norn.

"No!" Brynhildr shrieked. "What have you done?"

The magical barrier gave out causing the Valkyrie to pitch forward. Realizing she could join the fight, Brynhildr rushed straight for Skuld. In a heartbeat, she put all of her strength into punching Skuld in the face.

Skuld staggered backward from the blow. Her nose exploded with pain and her eyes watered.

The next punch connected with her left cheekbone. Ringing erupted in her ears and her vision blacked out. Unable to see and needing to protect herself, Skuld stumbled backward trying to get out of range.

Brynhildr swept Skuld's feet, sending the Norn tumbling backward onto the hard ground. As fast as thought, the Valkyrie leapt on top of her quarry, punching her face over and over again. She knew if she let up, then Skuld would retaliate and gain the upper hand.

As Brynhildr perched on her chest and pinned down her arms with her knees, Skuld tried to keep her wits about her while a constant barrage of punches connected with her face. Desperate to get the Valkyrie away from her, she traced a set of runes in the air along the edge of Brynhildr's leg activating a bubble of weightlessness. It was supposed to encompass only the Valkyrie, but the beating that she took impacted the application. Both of them floated into the air like feathers within what appeared to be a soap bubble.

With Brynhildr no longer restraining her, Skuld lashed out at the girl, striking her across the face.

Brynhildr took the hit and with a guttural shriek, she dove once again for Skuld. She managed to wrap her hands around the Norn's neck. Feeling the tightening of her attacker's grip, Skuld drew another spell, this time on herself. When the runes activated, sharp, curved iron spikes protruded from her skin. They punctured Brynhildr's hands. The Valkyrie snarled and tightened her grip, ignoring the searing pain.

"Enough!" Óðinn shouted. His large, rough hands

pierced through the spell bubble and grabbed hold of both of the women by the backs of their tunics. He held them at arm's length even as they struggled against his grasp.

Glaring at the Norn, Óðinn repeated, "You took my eye."

The Norn scowled back at him. "Yes, I did."

"Why?"

"The price for the knowledge has been paid. You may now drink from the Well of Wisdom."

"I do not take kindly to being disfigured," he said.

Skuld shrugged. "You intended to trade your eye before you knew Mímir lay dying. You merely gave it to me instead."

"You took it without cause or provocation."

Skuld crossed her arms over her chest as she dangled a few feet in the air in Óðinn's grip. The spikes she enchanted upon herself vanished. "It is written you trade your eye for a drink from the Well of Wisdom. This fate cannot be changed, One Eye. To change such a thing is inviting your very own destruction."

Óðinn considered her words thoughtfully. "It is written on the tree that I give my eye for knowledge?" he asked.

"It is," Skuld affirmed. "Put me down. I only sought to ensure the events of fate were met. I will do no more harm."

"All it would take is one well-placed blade for me to be sure of that."

"Choose how to channel your anger wisely, One Eye. You want me on your side, remember?"

Trembling with contained rage, Óðinn set both Norn and Valkyrie down.

As soon as she returned to solid ground, Skuld traced the runes of healing over her face. It took away the cuts and bruises, though the memory of the pain still reverberated in her nerve endings. She bent to pick up her dagger before walking to the edge of the clearing to pick up the sword Týrfingr.

Brynhildr rushed to Óðinn to see the damage Skuld did first hand. The god shoved the young Valkyrie to the side. "I am fine, girl. Leave it be."

After sheathing her dagger and attaching the sword back onto her belt, Skuld straightened her cloak about her shoulders and whistled for Strix. The owl descended from a nearby tree, settling in his customary place on her shoulder.

"Time to leave, Strix."

As Óðinn and Brynhildr talked in low, urgent tones, Skuld walked out of the clearing. She hoped this episode would be the end of the fight. After all, she did what she had to do in order to keep the cycle progressing forward. She had not lied when she told Óðinn that not giving up his eye would lead to his downfall.

At the very least, what happened should have dissuaded Óðinn from making Brynhildr follow her.

That hope faded when, after a while of walking, she heard heavy footfalls crunching through the snow behind her. They followed at a distance, as though hesitant to fully walk with her.

Heaving a sigh, Skuld halted her purposeful stride. Luck was not on her side. Now she would have to deal with a persistent and angry Valkyrie. If Brynhildr still followed after the fight they just had, then the Norn wasn't sure what other actions she could take to deter the girl.

The footsteps stopped a few yards away from where Skuld waited. Annoyed, she called out, "Why are you following me? I thought you would want to stay with your foster father and wage war against the evil Vanir."

"You ripped his eye out," she replied.

Skuld shrugged. "It's the price he always pays."

The girl's brow furrowed. "What does that mean?"

Skuld turned to address Brynhildr face to face. "It

means in all of the cycles of Yggdrasil, he always exchanges his eye for a drink from the Well of Wisdom. It is fated and something which cannot be changed."

Brynhildr thought about this for a moment and gave a reluctant sigh. "If it was fated, then he could not avoid it."

Her reaction came as a surprise to Skuld. Uncertainly she asked, "You are not angry with me?"

The girl's tone took on a dangerous edge. "I'm furious with you. If I had my way, you would be floating face down in the well back there."

"Then why are you here?"

"If what you say is true and Óðinn's destiny was to give up his eye, then there's no sense fighting it. In fact, I think it's even more important I come with you now that I understand who you are."

"You mean that's what Óðinn wants," Skuld corrected. "I am not stupid, Brynhildr. I know he wants you to keep an eye on me."

The Valkyrie grit her teeth. "If you know then why bother asking me?"

Skuld didn't have a response to that. Instead, she walked in silence towards the river, wishing that she could leave the palpable tension in the air behind them.

After a few miles of tense and silent travel, Brynhildr asked, "Where are we going anyway?"

"We are going to Vanaheimr."

Brynhildr stopped in her tracks. "What? No. We can't go there. The Æsir are days away from waging war with the Vanir. Why would you want to go into their territory?"

Skuld glanced back, not at all surprised at Brynhildr's reticence. "Because that's what Mímir said before he died. Vanaheimr. Someone there knows what is happening to Yggdrasil. Someone there may even be responsible for all of this, including Mímir's death. The answers rest with the Vanir."

Chapter Six: Vanaheimr

Skuld regarded the rushing water of the Ífingr River. If she remembered the connections between the realms correctly then this river flowed into the sea which separated Ásgarðr and Vanaheimr.

"What are you doing? You shouldn't be so close to the water! It's dangerous!" Brynhildr called from farther up the bank. Fear punctuated every syllable as she hugged her body to the cliff face as though the very water would come up and swallow her whole.

"This is the fastest way to Vanaheimr," Skuld answered, scanning the bank for some sort of vessel. Anything would do. It just needed to be sturdy enough to make a short journey across down this river and across the sea it fed into.

"Why do we need the fastest way? Why can't we take our time and head over the mountains?"

The fear radiating off of the girl annoyed Skuld. "The water isn't going to hurt you, silly girl. Come here."

With great reticence, Brynhildr inched closer to Skuld, her feet treading cautiously over rocks and ice. "You know, Óðinn helped me sew up my swan suit last night after you fell asleep. I can fly again. We don't need to bother with sailing."

"Can you carry me as well?" Skuld asked. She watched the frown deepen on the young woman's face and received the answer she suspected.

Pressing the issue, she asked, "Have you ever been to Vanaheimr? Do you know how to get there over the mountains?"

A flush of anger and embarrassment shaded Brynhildr's cheeks as she retorted, "It's not like you've sailed there either. Don't you Nornir have special doorways you travel through?"

Skuld scoffed. "Believe me, if I could get to them then I'd happily do so. The fact remains there is no other way that will get us to Vanaheimr faster than the water." She turned her back on the girl to once again peer down into the fast-moving water.

"Maybe there's something we can use up river. Strix, will you go look?"

The owl took flight, soaring over the fast-moving river.

The roar of the rapids muffled a panicked yelp. Before Skuld could turn to see what happened, something crashed into her from behind. Earsplitting, panicked cries and wildly flailing arms, made Skuld stumble. Loose rocks shifted under her feet and fell into the river making her slip further.

Entangled and off-balance, the two plunged into the icy water. The shock of the cold-stunned Skuld as did the abrupt and hard connection with the rocks dwelling just beneath the surface. The current swept them downstream in a haphazard tumble. Skuld fought to breathe against the weight of the terrified and scrambling Valkyrie.

Brynhildr splashed in a panic trying desperately to cling to Skuld as though she were the only thing between her and death. Her frantic kicking and twisting against the current served to prevent Skuld from helping and merely staying afloat.

In the agonizing moments where she fought to gain gasps of breath before Brynhildr drug her underwater, Skuld considered pushing the Valkyrie away. *Let her drown*, she thought. *Get yourself to safety. It is more important to save Yggdrasil.* She could almost feel her numbed fingers releasing their grip on the girl willingly.

Though it tempted her, Skuld banished the treacherous thoughts. Brynhildr's fate did not lie at the bottom of the Ífingr River nor washed out to sea. The snatches of what would be Brynhildr's life as she had seen it when they first met floated in Skuld's mind. As irritating as the Valkyrie could be, she had saved Skuld multiple times on her journey. Brynhildr proved herself to be a good person, despite the recent fight they were both still angry about. From what Skuld saw of the Nine Realms, they could stand to have more good people in them, not less.

With her mind made up, Skuld renewed her fight to pin down the Valkyrie's arms so she could break through the surface to take in a much-needed breath. She couldn't allow Brynhildr's panic to infect her; that would be the best way for them both to drown. Skuld struggled to keep both of their heads above the freezing water. Even as furiously as she swam, her limbs succumbed to the numbness of the icy water. She couldn't feel her body anymore. Every so often, she heard Brynhildr's loud but short gasp for air and then the deafening noise of water pushing her head underneath once again.

Out of the corner of her eye, Skuld spotted a shining boat not far upriver. What the sight meant didn't quite register right away. She barely heard the shouts coming from it over the roar of the rapids. The current picked up speed and it took all of her concentration to avoid the rocks in their way.

Strong arms wrapped around her middle and pulled her backward. The sensation brought a fresh wave of fear. What grabbed her? Should she fight? Not sure what was happening, Skuld clutched at Brynhildr and gulped in air while she had a chance. The Valkyrie no longer thrashed and kicked, making it easier to keep hold of her.

When Skuld caught her breath enough to open her eyes, she saw the bobbing riverbank moving opposite of the current. The arms around her let go only to be replaced by a thick rope looping around herself and Brynhildr. Someone rescued them. Skuld was never so grateful or so terrified. Tilting her head, she tried to get a glimpse of her rescuer. The water obscured her view, but she managed to catch sight of a lithe golden-haired man.

The boat she'd seen earlier turned out to be closer than she thought. By the direction in which her savior swam, it would be their destination. The water became calmer and her heart wasn't beating so hard in her chest, so this time Skuld heard the splash as the man hoisted himself out of the water and onto the deck of the boat. The rope around her began to tug. As she and Brynhildr were hoisted upwards, the loops around her pinched her skin and bit into her flesh uncomfortably. They reached the railing and were pulled onto the deck, soaked and shivering.

Through numbed hands, Skuld felt the solid wood of the deck beneath her. Relief coursed through her and she allowed herself a moment to press her forehead to the deck in gratefulness. Breathing hard, she glanced over to her companion sure she would see the same thankful smile on the Valkyrie's face.

Brynhildr wasn't moving. Her skin became pale and her lips were tinged blue.

"Brynhildr?" Skuld called, her voice hoarse and no louder than a whisper. A strange fluttering feeling blossomed in her chest. Dismay and fear overrode her instincts and she scrambled on her hands and knees over to grab hold of the girl.

As though the man understood the terror clenching at Skuld's heart, he strode over to the lifeless Valkyrie and leaned over her prone form. Gently removing the girl from Skuld's arms, he adjusted her so she rested on her back. He straightened her head and brought his ear to her chest. His mouth twitched into a frown, not liking what he heard or didn't hear. With quick, successive movements proceeded to rip the sopping wet clothing off of her.

Before Skuld could protest, the stranger released the laces of the leather armor encasing Brynhildr's torso. With his hands on her chest, he pumped steadily before pinching her nose and pressing his mouth against hers.

"What are you doing?" Skuld demanded. The adrenaline that flooded through her to keep herself and Brynhildr alive tapered off, leaving her weak and trembling and unable to stop the man from this strange assault.

He ignored Skuld, his focus on the ritual he performed on the young woman. After the third repetition, Brynhildr coughed and sputtered, spitting out the lungful of water she had taken in from the river.

As she gasped and shuddered, the stranger helped to shift her onto her side.

"Don't sit up," he advised as he rubbed her back briskly. His voice sounded soft and warm. "You'll pass out again if you move too quickly. Stay there and rest a moment." Looking at Skuld with amber-hued eyes, he said, "Watch her. I'll get some blankets for you two."

He bounced to his feet and moved across the small deck to a couple of large wooden chests resting against the opposite wall of the boat. He rummaged around inside of one until he brought out two thick quilts. Bringing them back to where Skuld and Brynhildr shivered and coughed, he gave one to each and then helped Brynhildr sit all the way up against the railing.

"You should remove those wet clothes. They will freeze to you in this wind. The only way you're going to get warm is to completely dry off," he said.

The promise of warmth propelled Skuld to disrobe as fast as she could. With shaking hands, she set aside her weapons and her water-logged pack. It took longer to remove her trousers and her tunic, but when they were gone, she wrapped the dry quilt around her shoulders.

The sound of flapping wings preceded Strix's arrival. He landed on the railing of the ship, tilting his head curiously at Skuld.

"Don't ask," she muttered.

Brynhildr struggled with her partially undone clothing. Her arms shook as she tried to remove the sopping wet clothes. Patiently, their rescuer assisted, with the rest of the armor and her boots. Blushing, Brynhildr motioned him away when he tried to help with her tunic. Giving a slight inclination of his head, the man instead covered her with a blanket so she could undress with some modesty.

"Who are you?" Skuld rasped as she shivered against the feel of the fabric.

The stranger smiled brightly at them. "I am Skírnir, the loyal and trusted elven messenger of Freyr." He gave a brief bow. "Whom do I have the pleasure of rescuing?"

Skuld opened her mouth to answer, but her companion interrupted.

"I'm Brynhildr. Thank you for saving me, Skírnir. It was very noble of you. I've never met an elf before."

"Yes, thank you," Skuld agreed, wondering why Brynhildr gazed so longingly at Skírnir or why she blushed, even more, when he smiled back at her. "You say you are Freyr's messenger?"

Skírnir nodded. "Yes, I am. I'm sorry, I didn't quite catch your name."

"My name is Skuld. Tell me, Skírnir, are you heading to Vanaheimr, by chance?"

A faint glimmer of recognition sparkled in the elf's amber eyes when she gave her name. "As fate would have it," he answered with a knowing smile, "yes I am."

Brynhildr piped up through chattering teeth, "That's where we are going too!"

Skírnir raised an eyebrow at the young woman. "Is

that what you were doing splashing around in the river?"

Brynhildr flushed a deep red, embarrassed by the reminder of almost drowning.

Skírnir laughed good-naturedly at the girl. "Well, since we are all bound for Vanaheimr and since I've got a boat, I suppose the charitable thing to do is to bring you along with me."

"Why would you do that?" Skuld asked.

"It's not every day one has the pleasure of rescuing a Norn and a Valkyrie, much less the opportunity to escort them to Vanaheimr. My lady Freyja has long been expecting you."

Skuld blinked. "Freyja?"

"Yes, she is Freyr's twin sister. It would be my honor to introduce you."

The news someone, even a Vanir goddess, expected her for some time when she'd just decided to go to Vanaheimr disturbed Skuld. Fate was in an upheaval and even she could not discern what would happen. How could Freyja have such insight then? The information made Skuld's stomach turn with unease.

As Skírnir went to pull the anchor, Brynhildr leaned in to whisper to Skuld. "I am still mad at you. But it's cold. Huddle with me for warmth." The Valkyrie didn't wait for a response; she sidled up close to Skuld. Through the blankets, Skuld felt the violence of Brynhildr's shaking. In a moment of compassion, the Norn wrapped her arms around the girl.

"I am sorry you are still mad," she said. "I had no intention of making you angry. But I had to do what I did. Your foster father is an integral part of the cycle of the Nine Realms. It's vital for the health of Yggdrasil that things stay as much the same as possible despite what may be going wrong."

The comment piqued Brynhildr's interest. "What do you mean? What's wrong with Yggdrasil?"

Skírnir, keeping his eyes on the water ahead, called

out to his two guests, "When you've both dried off a bit, there's some dry clothes in the other trunk. I've got nothing suitable for ladies such as yourselves, but if you don't object to male style clothing while your things dry I think you would be more comfortable and warm."

The two women looked at each other. Brynhildr shrugged. "Dry clothes would be a blessing right now."

"Alright. Stay here. I don't want you to be pitched overboard," Skuld said as she shakily inched her way over to the giant chests. Now that they were out of the water, the air seemed so much colder.

As she moved, Skuld watched their host pull the anchor into the boat and then dash over to the rudder. Without the anchor keeping the boat in place, it lurched into motion with the sheer power of the river carrying it downstream.

Skírnir expertly maneuvered the small vessel around the rapids and the rocks. His deftness indicated he'd been down this particular river many times before.

"How long will it take for us to reach Vanaheimr?" Skuld inquired. The tilting of the boat made her clutch to the chest's lid to prevent it from falling on her. Even without standing, imbalance threatened her. Glancing at the Valkyrie, she noticed even the girl gripped the railing to stay seated upright.

Skírnir shrugged. "If the weather holds fair, it will take a day, maybe two. Longer if there's a squall out on the sea."

Skuld said nothing as she gathered the clothes and made her way back to Brynhildr.

When she was close enough to grab ahold of the railing as well, she tossed over a shirt and some trousers. "Here. These looked the warmest."

Brynhildr seized the clothing and, under the warm cover of the blanket, she put them on. She huddled in them, wrapping the excess fabric tightly around her body to capture more of the warmth. She kept stealing furtive glances at Skírnir and blushing even more whenever he looked back at her.

Skuld changed as well, leaving her wet clothes in a pile on the deck. The men's tunic and trousers were indeed warm, though oversized. She used her belt to keep the trousers up and rolled the sleeves to the tunic so they weren't covering her hands.

The roughness of the river guaranteed both Skuld and Brynhildr stayed in their spot near the railing. Strix took to the air and followed the ship. The motion of the boat, however, turned Skuld's stomach and a peculiar throbbing started in her head. The cold wind on her face became a welcomed thing. She tilted her face to the sky, using the airflow to control her nausea.

"So are you going to tell me what is wrong with Yggdrasil?" Brynhildr asked. Her eyes were fixed on Skírnir; the wind whipped his golden hair backward and the sun shone on his tanned face. A nimbus of light seemed to surround him, making him difficult to look at without concentrated effort.

"I hadn't intended to," Skuld replied.

The Valkyrie pressed, "You owe me an explanation. I watched you disfigure the All-Father. What's more, we are heading straight into enemy territory. I think I deserve to know why."

A long, exacerbated sigh escaped Skuld's lips. It didn't seem worth the fight to continue hiding her purpose from the Valkyrie any longer. Since there was no getting rid of her at this point, it might help to have her understand what the stakes were.

"Yggdrasil is sick. Someone befouled the Well of Destiny by murdering a friend of mine in its waters. The murderer got away and I am hunting for them. Hopefully, once we catch this person, my sisters and I can put things right and heal the great tree. If we don't, well, it will be the end of everyone and everything in the Nine Realms."

Brynhildr frowned and glanced over at Skuld. "I

don't understand. Nornir control fate. Why didn't you just undo the destiny?"

"I couldn't. There's certain things that happen in the realm-cycle which cannot be changed."

"You mean like Óðinn losing his eye? You said it had to happen."

"Yes, that's right. Those things I cannot change. However, because Yggdrasil is sick, it is throwing everything out of balance. Things are happening which shouldn't. That's why it is so important the events that are fixed continue to happen as they should. If they do not, then it could throw things even more out of balance and it might accelerate the death of our home. For the first time, there are things my sisters and I haven't seen in this cycle. This culprit's fate is unknown to me."

"And you think the person who murdered your friend also murdered Mímir?"

"Yes, it appears to be the case. Vanaheimr is the best lead I have to capture them. Then I will leave the realms and see if my sisters and I can fix this mess."

A thought occurred to Brynhildr and she grew pale. "You don't think Skírnir's the one who . . ."

Skuld shrugged. "Could be, but I don't think so. Why would the murderer rescue us from the river?"

Brynhildr took in all of this information somberly. She was so quiet that Skuld fought the urge to ask what she thought.

When the silence stretched out to uncomfortable lengths, Brynhildr spoke. "It's so strange hearing a Norn talk about changing fate. We humans in Miðgarðr are raised with the belief that our destinies are unchangeable no matter what we do. We believe when our time is done in the realm of the living, then our runes were carved that way. We never question the predetermination of our lives."

Skuld shrugged, "They are set for the most part. There are minor things here and there which my sisters and I adjust, but from birth to death, your paths are carved into the tree."

The Valkyrie nodded, deep in her thoughts. "So you know what will happen to me. You know what destiny awaits me." It wasn't a question, but rather an affirmation.

"I do. But I will not tell you about it. For now, know that your name and your deeds will be sung about for generations after you are gone. Assuming, of course, my sisters and I can set things right."

"Thank you for telling me," Brynhildr said. "I'm still angry about what you did to Óðinn, but I think I understand it better."

"You're welcome," Skuld replied. She watched the girl gather up their wet clothes and crawl over to where the sun shone the strongest to lay them out.

"Skírnir," Brynhildr called, eager to make a good impression on him. "What can you tell me about Álfheimr? I've never been there before."

Skuld huddled on the deck, trying not to be sick from the constant motion. She listened to Brynhildr ask Skírnir all sorts of questions, most of which struck her as inane. Why did the young woman need to know about Álfheimr or what each part of the boat was called? She watched the two of them interact with a mounting unease in her chest. They didn't know Skírnir at all. With his connections to the Vanir, why would she latch onto someone like that? Perhaps because he was an elf? Skuld had heard human women were often quite taken with elves.

A sudden jerk of the boat and the choppiness of the water upheaved the contents of Skuld's stomach. Instinctively, she turned her head over the side of the boat just in time for the vomit to come spewing out of her mouth.

Her retching drew the attention of both Skírnir and Brynhildr.

"Oh no, Skuld!" Brynhildr cried.

"Here, take this horn and get her some water from the barrel near the mast." Skírnir tossed Brynhildr a polished cattle horn cup. She did as the sailor said, spilling more than half of it as she staggered around the deck to get to where Skuld hung over the rail. She gripped the edge of the boat and handed Skuld the horn.

"Drink this," she said, sympathetically and rubbed Skuld's back for comfort.

"You're just seasick. You'll get better over time," Skírnir promised. "You will also learn to get your sea legs and be able to walk without falling. It just takes some time. Drink the water. It will help."

The swift-moving current of the river deposited them into a great sea with dark water cresting in large waves. Expertly, Skírnir navigated through the breakers and took the small vessel out to the middle of the water where the land of Jǫtunheimr and Ásgarðr were mere smudges in the distance.

The advice Skírnir gave turned out to be accurate enough, for Brynhildr. Surprisingly, the aquaphobic Valkyrie took to sailing naturally. Within hours of her rescue, she'd mastered the art of walking along the deck without falling. Skuld watched on with ever-increasing sea sickness.

If Skuld thought sailing down the river was bad, then the sea was horrific. With nothing to steady her gaze on, everything shifted and pitched with the ocean currents. Her stomach roiled along with the sharp tides and all she could do between bouts of vomiting was close her eyes and sip from the horned cup Brynhildr filled with fresh water for her.

For the entire journey, Skuld clung to the edge of the boat, with her eyes closed and wishing she were dead. Often Strix perched near her and pecked at her hair as though trying to comfort her. While the young Valkyrie had the time of her life enjoying the attentions of Skírnir,

Skuld rued her decision to sail to Vanaheimr.

After what seemed like an eternity at sea, mountains appeared at the edges of the horizon. Something shimmered against the backdrop of hope, almost like glass reflecting light. Skírnir gave a shout of happiness as he and Brynhildr set about rowing towards what Skuld considered to be her favorite part about the Nine Realms; solid earth beneath her feet.

"Is that Vanaheimr?" she asked Skírnir as they rowed.

"That's the fjord leading into it," he answered. "You will be on land again before nightfall."

The shimmer in the air didn't move as they got closer. In fact, Skuld noticed the landscape became less and less distinct the closer they got.

Skírnir didn't pay any attention to the wall of glass and faceted fractals of light. He and Brynhildr rowed the boat right through it without a second glance.

However, as soon as they passed through, what Skuld had mistaken as an outline of impressive mountains and narrow inlets solidified to an incredible view. Before her eyes, everything shifted. The mountains became a series of rolling hills and valleys. An abundance of plants and wild animals could be seen even from their vantage point from the sea. Along the beach stood an impressive settlement of structures and several docks jutting out into the water.

Before they got any closer, another smaller boat came up alongside the stern. An old, weathered man with windswept gray hair and a matching beard waved from his position at his rudder.

The captain of Skuld's boat waved back affably.

"Fair weather, Njǫrðr."

"Fair weather, indeed, Skírnir. It is good to see you again. I trust you have good news for my son?"

Skírnir smiled. "I may."

Njǫrðr returned the smile, his astute gray eyes

drawn to where Skuld and Brynhildr sat at the oars. "I notice you have some guests. Who are you bringing into Vanaheimr unannounced?"

"Not unannounced. Your daughter Freyja is expecting them. This is Skuld and Brynhildr."

The Vanir sailing god glowered at the elf. His hand went to his spear. "A Valkyrie? Skírnir, we are at war with the Æsir and you bring one of Óðinn's Valkyries to our doorstep? Have you gone out of your elvish mind?"

Sensing the diplomatic nightmare upon them, Brynhildr stepped forward. "Yes, I am one of Óðinn's Valkyries, but I am not here because of the war. I am Skuld's bodyguard to ensure her safety. I intend no harm."

Njǫrðr pursed his lips, his dislike for the situation plain. He looked at Skírnir. "Are you sure my daughter is expecting them?"

The messenger nodded. "She is. I wouldn't delay them much longer than they already are." The man leaned forward nearer to Njǫrðr and whispered, "You know how she can be."

The reminder of his daughter's temperament made Njǫrðr's frown even deeper. "Aye, I know. Do you vouch for them, Skírnir? They won't cause any trouble while they are guests in Vanaheimr?"

Skírnir nodded solemnly. "They shall be the perfect guests. I give you my word."

That seemed to satisfy the old god. "Alright then. Off with you three. I have a port to run."

Grinning, Skírnir motioned for the two women to start rowing towards an open dock.

The main port of Vanaheimr appeared to be a bustling place. Several ships and boats crowded the docks as goods were simultaneously loaded and unloaded from the berths of the dragon-headed vessels. An urgency hung in the air, a tension that seemed to echo off of the fjords along with every terse shout and order from the people carting heavy loads. The lowing of sheep and goats punctuated the din of rolling barrels and heavy sacks being slung onto planks.

Skírnir guided the boat to an empty dock at the innermost part of the harbor with practiced familiarity. After tying the boat securely, the elf helped both Brynhildr and Skuld disembark.

Having spent days with nothing but the bobbing and swaying of water beneath her, the stationary firmness of the dock was abrupt and disorienting. It took more than a few steps to remember how to walk on solid ground. Strix waited until she got her balance before landing on her arm.

Brynhildr stumbled after her and it gave Skuld a perverse satisfaction that the Valkyrie had just as much trouble as she.

"Welcome to Vanaheimr," Skírnir said as he led the way off of the dock and into what appeared to be a bustling marketplace. "Before I take you to Freyja, we need to get you two cleaned up and presentable. The lady is very discerning of her visitors. Luckily, I already have a gift you can present to her. It should hasten our arrival at her hall."

"What sort of gift?" Brynhildr asked. Her eyes were wide as she took in all of the people going about their business.

"Golden bracelets I had made in Álfheimr. Lady Freyja has a weakness for golden jewelry. She will be delighted when you present them to her."

Skuld halted in the middle of the busy marketplace. Several Vanir citizens brushed past her, muttering their annoyance. "You got her the gift before you found us in the river. Did you find us on purpose?"

Skírnir made a point not to answer the Norn. "Look!" he gasped, changing the subject. "A bathhouse! That is just what you two need."

"We don't have time for this," Skuld said, irritated

the elf dismissed her question.

"We do because I refuse to bring esteemed visitors to my lady looking like they were half-drowned. It isn't done. Now, go on and get cleaned up. I will return with suitable attire for both of you by the time you are finished."

Skírnir all but pushed Skuld and Brynhildr towards the bathhouse.

"Come on, Skírnir's right. We both need a bath." Brynhildr tugged at Skuld's oversized sleeve.

The Norn relented, though she grumbled about the delay under her breath. "Best wait for us out here," she told her owl companion.

The bathhouse was an old stone building filled with steam. Servants scrubbed the grime of travel from the two women. Both Skuld's black hair and Brynhildr's reddish-gold tresses were anointed with oils and done up in intricate braids. Skuld didn't know what sort of oil they used, but the smell of it made her nose itch with its cloying intensity. She hoped Freyja didn't have a sense of smell, otherwise, the stench of her person would run the goddess out of the room.

By the time they were ready to dress, Skírnir slipped their newly purchased clothing to the servants assisting them. The dresses and accessories Skírnir selected were a definite departure from their usual armor and traveling cloaks, but presumably more befitting the culture around them.

Skuld hated the swaying skirts and too tight laces. She insisted on keeping her dagger and Týrfingr on her belt. As a result, her fine green dress with golden embroidered edges clashed with her leather belt. The rest of her gear had been packed in a new woven bag.

Brynhildr, showing solidarity with Skuld, also refused to surrender her sword, though her sheath looked more elegant against her blue gown. The fabric matched the brightness of her eyes. Her swan suit found its way into its own bag.

"Now you are ready to be presented," Skírnir told them, beaming with pride when they emerged from the bathhouse. "Come, I will have a chariot take us to the hall." He motioned for them to follow as he made his way down the street towards a nearby stable.

"Isn't this exciting?" Brynhildr whispered to Skuld. "I have never had such fine things. I'll wager I've never looked so beautiful before either. Did you hear how Skírnir complimented the color of my dress? Just like cornflowers, he said."

The gushing annoyed Skuld. "Stop it," she said as she patted Strix's head. "You are acting like a fool. We can't forget why we are here. We can't afford to put our guard down."

The reminder sobered the young Valkyrie. "Right."

At that moment, Skírnir returned to the ladies. "Our wagon awaits. Freyja will be very excited to see you."

Skuld and Brynhildr exchanged wary glances and followed Skírnir to a small wagon drawn by a single horse. Skírnir, ever the gentleman, helped both Brynhildr and Skuld into the back of the wagon where cushioned seats made the journey more comfortable. Skírnir himself took hold of the reins and with a click of his tongue, the three were off.

Skuld watched with interest as the landscape changed from bustling market and port to rolling fields dotted by patches of trees. Outside of town were several crops, a testament to the fertile land Vanaheimr was famed for. Crops of grains, root vegetables, even a few apple orchards soon gave way to wild grasses and thickets. The smell of growing things permeated the air. Where Ásgarðr appeared to be in autumn, Vanaheimr reveled in the height of summer.

"You know, when I left here a week ago, winter had just begun to set in," Skírnir said as they rolled down the path. "In Álfheimr, they started their planting. Something strange is happening in the realms from what I can see."

"What do you think it is?" Brynhildr asked as she gave Skuld a meaningful look.

Skírnir sighed, "I wish I knew."

The homes in Vanaheimr were made of wood and turf with thatched roofs. Horses grazed on the abundant pastures. Skuld found the farther away from the bustle of the market, the more serene and peaceful the atmosphere became. It felt as though a spell had been placed on the very air she breathed to make her feel calm.

"There it is," Skírnir said, breaking the peaceful silence. "Freyja's hall." He pointed off to the left of the path to a long house twice as large, but otherwise not unlike the others they saw along the way. What made the turf and thatched house stand out was the set of golden double doors shining in the sunlight. Those doors belonged in a palace, not what appeared to be a layman's home.

Brynhildr's hand found Skuld's and squeezed it in silent reassurance. The gesture made Skuld's lips twitch in a small smile. Even with how annoying the Valkyrie could be, she was glad of Brynhildr's presence.

Skírnir pulled the wagon around to the side of the hall just beyond a steep woodpile. As the two women helped each other out, Skírnir unhitched the horse and led it to a nearby corral. When he circled back, both women had smoothed their dresses and adjusted their weapons. They were ready to meet the goddess.

Chapter Seven: Seiðr

Whatever Skuld expected a domicile of a goddess to be, her imagination failed her. The large, golden double doors opened to a darkened hall. It took Skuld's eyes a moment to adjust to the dimmed lighting. When she could see, it took everything in her not to gasp at the sheer luxury before her.

Every inch of the hall was a barrage against the senses. Dozens of candles created a warm glow that illuminated the space. Tapestries of red and gold covered the walls, making the room seem smaller and more intimate. Treasures and fine art littered tables and shelves. The candlelight reflected off of their polished surfaces. Thick ornamented braziers were spaced every few feet, adding to the candles' illumination and diffusing an exotic scent from the spices and herbs smoldering in their bowls. Skuld found the aroma strangely comforting; it summoned images of warm sunny days in fields of blossoming flowers. The hardwood floors were covered in furs and thick carpets, making each step feel as though they were walking on top of clouds.

A soft meow drew Skuld's attention downward. At her feet, a large, fluffy orange cat stared back up at her.

"Look, Skuld!" Brynhildr whispered in an odd, high-pitched voice. "A cat!" The Valkyrie picked up a similar-looking orange cat and hugged it to her face. "It's so soft!"

"Put the cat down," Skuld admonished.

Brynhildr scowled at the Norn and kept cuddling the animal. "He likes me." As the words came out of her mouth, more cats approached, emerging from hiding places all over the hall. Their coloring varied, ranging from solid black, to calico, and everything in between. Skuld counted at least nine, but there might have been more. The din of their meows filled the room. Strix hooted and ruffled his feathers, not appreciating the feline presence.

"Who dares to come into my hall unannounced?" a sultry, feminine voice demanded from the farthest reaches of the hall. Skuld couldn't see who spoke as they were concealed by a section of curtains at the back of the room.

Skírnir stepped forward. "My lady, it is I, Skírnir, returned from the mission to Álfheimr your brother bade me to go on."

"Skírnir," the voice lost it's harsh, commanding done and gained a softer, more indulgent familiarity. "You return to us. Tell me, was your journey successful?"

"Yes, my lady, though the path to Álfheimr grows more and more turbulent. I fear the realm will soon be unattainable from the river."

"I see. We shall have to find another way to connect with our elvish allies. I am sure you and my brother will come up with something."

"Yes, my lady. I've also brought you the visitors you have been expecting."

A weary sigh emanated from the curtains, just loud enough for the visitors to hear the agitation.

"I am not fit for company, Skírnir. Send them away."

Skírnir gave the two women an apologetic smile. "But my lady, they are here and I do believe you have been expecting one of them for quite some time now."

"How dare you bring them in here without my consent!" the goddess raged. Intending to tell her uninvited guests to leave, she twitched back the curtains and froze when she saw the glowering dark-haired Norn and the confused, but forcedly smiling Valkyrie.

Skuld eyed the goddess, striving to keep her face neutral. She had been right in not wanting company. Her skin was burnt and blackened, though spots of it were healing into a violent scarlet hue which tamed to a puckered, but pale white. Her burnished bronze hair, uneven and brittle, grew back in clumps on her pink scalp.

Brynhildr, however, didn't have the same common sense to keep quiet about her hostess's appearance. Without thinking, the Valkyrie exclaimed, "By the grace of Þórr's goats, what in all the Nine Realms happened to you?"

Freyja's expression of surprise morphed into a dangerous scowl. "This is the result of an encounter with the Æsir, young Valkyrie. The gods you align yourself with burned, raped, and tortured me. Take heed when dealing with your master so this does not happen to you."

Brynhildr's eyes widened and she shifted her weight from one foot to the other at the angry goddess's proclamation. "It can't. . . Are you also called Gullveig?"

"It is a name I use when traveling. Has your master spoken of me then? Tell me, what did he say to you?"

Skuld interjected, getting right to the heart of what she wanted to know. "We don't have time for this. How did you know I would be here?"

The question brought a knowing smile to the goddess's lips. With a flick of her eyes, Freyja dismissed Brynhildr and settled her gaze on Skuld. Instead of answering right away, she emerged from behind the curtain.

"Skírnir, thank you for delivering our guests. My brother is awaiting you at his hall. He wishes for you to meet him there."

The blonde messenger bowed. "Thank you, my lady." When he rose, he flashed a bright smile at Brynhildr before exiting.

When he left, Freyja moved further towards the center of the room and reclined on an elaborate cushioned and fur-lined throne.

"I've seen you in visions, but I didn't know for sure you would come. It is an honor to meet you, Skuld. Your journey must have been exhausting. May I offer you some refreshments?" She gestured to a couple of pillow festooned lounges near her own. "Please, be comfortable."

The two women glanced at each other but remained standing.

Freyja laughed at their caution. "I am not going to hurt you, you silly things. I just wish to speak with you."

They hesitated a moment longer before Skuld shrugged and moved to sit on one of the lounges. She came here for answers and it seemed playing Freyja's game, whatever it was, would be the only way to get what she needed. As soon as she took her seat, three cats jumped into her lap, a veritable weight of fluff that kept her pinned in place. Strix hooted irritably and ruffled his feathers even more. Skuld reached up to stroke his chest in an effort to soothe her friend.

Brynhildr paused, watching Freyja as though she couldn't decide if the goddess would attack or not. At last, she sat on the lounge next to Skuld. The Valkyrie had the presence of mind to dig into her pack to extract the golden bracelets Skírnir gave them as Freyja's gift.

"Please, take these bracelets as a thank you for your hospitality. We are humbled." She proffered them to the goddess in a formal and stiff manner.

A bemused smile crossed the too tight and singed face of Freyja as she reached out to take the golden circlets from the Valkyrie. "Hardly necessary, but I thank you all the same. They are quite lovely." After admiring them, Freyja deposited the two pieces of jewelry next to a small bell that sat on the arm of her throne.

Keeping her eyes on her guests, Freyja picked up the delicate bell and rang it.

From another doorway off to the side of the hall came a slender yet toned young man. He dressed conservatively enough in a richly embroidered belted tunic and thick woven trousers. His long reddish-blonde hair was braided back with golden string. Kohl lined his deep brown eyes, giving him an exotic appearance. He carried a golden tray laden with a jewel-encrusted pitcher and four matching goblets.

Freyja clapped her hands in delight. "Wonderful foresight! Evyndr, my dear, please, come sit with us awhile."

The young man sat opposite of Skuld and Brynhildr, setting the tray on the small table next to him. With careful, deliberate movements, he poured the contents of the pitcher into the goblets, handing one to each of the three women. He took the last one.

Skuld watched the man, all of the alarm bells going off in her head. The air around him buzzed and crackled with strange energies. The feel of it so close made her skin crawl and her head throb. The only thing that resonated in her mind was that Evyndr shouldn't be here. Skuld desperately wanted to use her runes to understand why she had such a visceral reaction to Evyndr's presence. But she couldn't; not with Freyja watching her like a cat watches a mouse. Later, then.

Noticing the scrutiny with which Skuld inspected the newcomer, Freyja said, "May I introduce you to my faithful advisor, Evyndr."

The man gave a solitary nod.

After a prodding nudge from the Valkyrie, Skuld broke her contemplative gaze from the strange man Evyndr and decided to just get on with the matter at hand.

"Skírnir said you were expecting me for some time." Skuld set her untouched mead on the table next to her lounge. "I don't see how that is possible since I only decided to come to Vanaheimr the day we met him. So, I ask you, Freyja, how is it that you have been expecting my visit?"

"She has not," Evyndr spoke up. "I have." He took a long sip from his goblet before putting it aside. "I saw you in a vision during a Seiðr. In the vision, you came to us asking for help."

Skuld frowned. "Seiðr?"

Evyndr tilted his head quizzically. "I am surprised you do not know the practice. It is the magic used to foresee the future, among other things."

Skuld lifted her chin, her eyes hard with suspicion. "I am not familiar with this art called Seiðr. It is my business to carve what ought to be into being. I do not see how you mortals can discern fate."

"You will not goad me, Norn," Freyja said, her lips curled in distaste. "I have practiced and taught the power of Seiðr most of my life. We have offered our help. You can either take it or not. It is your choice."

Skuld fought with herself over how much to tell them. Things were not right here. The presence of Evyndr, this promise they could see into the future when her own powers failed her, it all made her stomach lurch. Still, perhaps this is precisely what Mímir meant when he said Vanaheimr magic and rune-less fate.

Taking a deep breath, Skuld said, "I am looking for someone responsible for several great wrongs. I suspect they stole water from all of the three wells that nourish Yggdrasil. Most recently the Well of Wisdom. When we arrived there, we found Mímir drawing his last breaths. This cursed sword is a clue to finding the culprit." Skuld removed Týrfingr from her belt and showed it to the goddess and her advisor.

The smug smile disappeared from Freyja's healing face. Her relaxed, almost jovial stance stiffened in shock. "Mímir is dead?"

"Yes."

Freyja's eyes flitted to Evyndr and back to Skuld. "I had no idea about Mímir. And you believe the culprit to be here in Vanaheimr?"

Both Evyndr and Freyja leaned forward to get a good look at the sword.

"It's quite possible," Evyndr spoke up. His voice sounded deep and rich, like late summer honey. "Do you know who the sword belongs to?"

Skuld shook her head. "No. I suspect the original owners are long dead. I don't quite understand how it appeared in this cycle in the first place."

Evyndr mused, "There is a way for us to find out. The art of Seiðr is a most delicate undertaking. There is no guarantee you will get the answers you seek. However, what do you stand to lose?"

He had a point. Though doubt filled her, she asked in a low voice, "What do I need to do?"

Evyndr rose to his feet and bowed. "You need only ask the questions. I will begin the preparations and we will get started shortly."

"Wait," Brynhildr interjected. "Isn't Freyja going to do the Seiðr?"

The goddess gave the Valkyrie an irritated look as she gestured to her burned and healing face. "I am in no state for Seiðr magic. Evyndr is more than capable to perform the ceremony in my place."

Brynhildr shifted in her seat, suddenly uncomfortable. "I don't like this, Skuld," she said, keeping a hard eye on Evyndr.

An amused smile stretched Evyndr's lips upwards. "What's wrong, Brynhildr? Your Valkyrie training didn't prepare you for a little sorcery?"

The young Valkyrie glowered at the man. Never before had Skuld seen her so disgusted. "Men should not do woman's magic. It's not right."

Evyndr gave a playful wink to the distrustful

Valkyrie. "Right is relative to the side you are on," he said. "You may not approve, young warrior, but the best part is our methods don't require your approval."

"*Argr*," Brynhildr spat at him. Hatred thickened her voice and the abrupt accusation of effeminacy took Skuld by surprise.

Evyndr, for his part, laughed at the derogatory slur. "I can tell you are heavily influenced by your Æsir benefactors. Trust them to instill such staunch ideals of *drengr* and foolish manliness even in their Valkyrie women."

"You do realize your precious Óðinn is also considered *argr*," Freyja said. "His obsession with learning the magical arts and seeking out his knowledge does not stop when it comes to the womanly art of Seiðr. In fact, I taught him some of what he knows. I would have taught him more if he hadn't ordered his tribe of arrogant, dim-witted fighters to rape and murder me."

"That's a lie," Brynhildr argued, her voice rising with emotion. Her hand strayed to her sword hilt.

"Enough!" Skuld shouted getting holding her hands out. Strix fluttered to the rafters of the hall at her abrupt movement. "We are here to find out where the murderer is, not to argue about what is or is not shameful."

Her companion settled into an angry silence while her hostess and Evyndr exchanged sly smiles.

Evyndr said, "There are many things to prepare. I respectfully ask for your patience."

"While we wait, we shall feast," Freyja decided, her tone forcibly upbeat. "Brynhildr, I trust our food will not offend you?" The goddess got up from her chair and followed Evyndr out of the side door of the hall, presumably to where the kitchens were.

Brynhildr sat stiffly in her chair, unwilling to show the slightest hint of the roiling anger and confusion inside of her. When both Freyja and Evyndr left the room, Skuld put a reassuring hand on her knee.

"It's alright," she said. "Whatever is going to happen, you will be safe."

"It's not me I am worried about," Brynhildr replied. "I don't trust these people and it's not because they are Vanir. There's something not right about any of this. Why have you never heard of this ritual?"

Skuld had to admit she made a good point. However, instead of telling her that, Skuld said, "I understand, but if this can get me closer to capturing the person who murdered my friend and Mímir, then I will do it. You've made no such agreement. I know Óðinn made you come with me, but I am telling you that you are free to leave whenever you wish."

She meant the offer to be kind, but Brynhildr shoved Skuld's hand away from her. In an icy tone, she said, "You think so little of me, that I would go back on my word and abandon you here with these dangerous people?"

"I am still going to do this Seiðr, whether you agree or not."

The Valkyrie sighed in apparent defeat. "And I will be here to watch your back in case these witches decide to stab it."

As the two waited for their hostess and her strange advisor, three silent servants came into the hall. They wore simple, homespun shifts and scarves to cover their hair. The women didn't even acknowledge the guest's presence as they gathered the goblets of half-drunk mead. They picked up Freyja's throne and placed it atop a table. They placed a small step in front, forming a makeshift dais. The pelts, cushions, and woven blankets overflowed from the throne onto the table.

Having arranged the seat according to some unknown specification, the servants turned their attentions to where Brynhildr and Skuld sat.

"Please excuse us. We need to set up the table for the feast," one of them said.

Unsure of what else to do, Brynhildr and Skuld got

up and shuffled to a relatively safe spot near one of the tapestried walls. They watched as the serving women brought out a wooden table in sections. With practiced ease, they assembled the board and set it with fine golden plates and utensils. Thick white candles were brought to the center and lit, giving the room more light.

Their tasks completed, they retreated through the side doors, never even looking back at the strangers huddling against the wall.

Moments later, the servants returned bearing heavy food-laden platters. Three times they did this until the table brimmed with food.

"Who is going to eat all of this?" Brynhildr whispered to Skuld.

Skuld frowned. "This is the sign of a good host, isn't it? Is it not customary to offer guests food?

"Yes, but this isn't meant as hospitality. This is showing off."

"What does that mean?"

Brynhildr's lips pursed together as Freyja emerged robed in a sumptuous crimson and gold gown of elvish silk lined in white fur and with a full goblet in her hands. She gestured to the table. "Please, eat. It won't be long before Evyndr is ready."

Freyja settled herself on the lounge and, as she ladled some of the delicacies onto a golden plate, she once again turned to a gracious hostess. "Brynhildr, you are so young. Have you seen many battles?"

Following Skuld back to their seat at the table, the young Valkyrie answered, "I've seen enough to know what to do."

Skuld took a plate and started spooning a very small portion of food onto it. The memory of how sick she had been on the boat minimized her appetite.

Freyja watched her guests as she sipped from her goblet. She asked the Valkyrie, "What do you know of battle magic?"

Brynhildr shook her head noncommittally.

Freyja gave a deep, throaty laugh. "Surely Óðinn has warned his warriors about Vanir battle magic! How does he expect you to fight against it if he hasn't told you of what we are capable of?"

Brynhildr couldn't hide the revulsion on her face. "Óðinn told us plenty. You Vanir use trickery and backhanded ways to win a fight. From what I've heard, Vanir lack honor."

The goddess gave a dismissive wave of her hand. "Your talk of honor is laughable. Evyndr was right; you have been instilled with far too many *drengr* ideals. Is it not part of the *drengr* code to meet your enemy with all the skills you possess? Where is the honor in smashing shields together without a strategy or plan? Honor, dear girl, is a matter of opinion."

"I never said there wasn't a strategy involved," Brynhildr answered defensively. "I just mean one should not hide behind magic. If you are going to fight, it is better to do so face to face. No magic, no tricks, just one on one. The strongest will prevail."

"Agree to disagree." Freyja shrugged, the knowing smile still on her face. "In the end, the mightiest will win this war. A war started, by the way, by none other than Óðinn himself. You will understand soon enough your masters are not as honor-bound as you imagine them to be." She took a long drink from her goblet, spilling some down the front of her dress. The goddess wiped at the dampness with her hand.

Skuld grew impatient with the senseless barbs between Brynhildr and Freyja.

"How soon will this ritual be ready?" she asked to break up the conversation.

"It is ready now," Evyndr said from the doorway.

The trio of women turned at the sound of his voice. He stood at the edge of the room in full ritual garb. He wore a black dress and cape which sparkled from the many gems sewn into them. Covering his hands were blue gloves and Skuld thought she saw white cat fur at the inside edges. A matching blue hood with more cat skin sat atop his blonde curls. His feet were covered in shaggy calf-skin boots that laced up to his knees. In one hand he held a knobby staff inlaid with gems and brass. From leather strings, beads and charms dangled from the top of it. In his other hand, he held a taut calf-skin drum painted with runes and other mystical symbols.

A sharp intake of breath could be heard as he passed by Brynhildr and Skuld. The Valkyrie's cheeks reddened in embarrassment at witnessing a man dress as a woman.

For his part, Evyndr didn't seem to notice or care about the Valkyrie's discomfort. He strode up to the raised chair and climbed atop of it.

"We have little time to spare," Evyndr said, his voice taking on a thick, tenor quality. "We will begin with singing songs to invite the powers of fate to bless our ritual; present company notwithstanding, of course," Evyndr gave Skuld a nod.

Skuld remained skeptical. None of this was familiar to her and she suspected it was all an elaborate farce. Still, she kept silent as Evyndr cleared his throat and began beating the drum with his staff in a slow, but steady beat.

He drummed in silence for a few measures, making the sound echo in Skuld's chest. When the beat had been established, his voice rang out clear and powerful. Freyja herself joined in. Their haunting melody wove itself in and out of the drumbeats. The words were strange; not like anything Skuld heard before, which gave her pause. Were they really words or just nonsense?

The songs went on for quite some time. Brynhildr and Skuld watched Evyndr and Freyja sing and drum and experienced nothing while they did so. At last, the songs seemed to end and the drumming ceased.

"Thank you, Freyja, for lending your sweet voice to

the ritual," Evyndr said. He looked at Skuld and announced, "Fate is here with us. It has a message for you."

Skuld raised her eyebrow but remained silent.

Evyndr listened to the silence in the hall, tilting his head ever so slightly. "The one you seek is in Miðgarðr. A man named Angantýr."

"Angantýr," Skuld repeated. She didn't recall much about the person, but it sounded familiar. A sense of importance surrounded the name, however until she could reliably carve the runes, she could not know why. Unsure if she could trust the answers from the Seiðr ritual, Skuld decided to test it. "To make sure what you say is true, answer me this: how did Óðinn gain the wisdom of the runes?"

Evyndr remained perched on his seat, motionless as he answered in a monotone, "Óðinn sacrificed himself to himself and hung from the great tree for nine days and nine nights. The runes were his prize."

Skuld's surprise at hearing the truth made her blink. Óðinn's sacrifice hadn't occurred in this realm. Which meant whatever power answered her knew of the future.

She asked again, "Answer me this: how the Nine Realms will end."

"Ragnarǫk will tremble the worlds. Gods will fight and gods will die. Such is the way it always ends."

"Answer me this: what is the cursed blade I carry and how did it come to be cursed?"

"Týrfingr was forged by a dwarf and cursed by a dwarf. Three terrible tragedies are what it shall reap."

All of the answers were right. Still, Skuld found herself hesitant to trust Evyndr at his word. "Answer me this: for what purpose did I leave my home and enter into the Nine Realms?"

"To seek the stranger who stole the sacred well water and who intends to change the fate of the realms."

The last answer made Skuld curious. She guessed

the culprit stole the water, but the reasoning for it eluded her. The idea the perpetrator gathered the well water in order to change the fate of the realms struck her as dangerous. How could they be used in such a way?

Putting the question aside, Skuld asked one more. "Answer me this: how do you know Angantýr is the one we are looking for?"

"Ratatǫskr's blood on his hands. The Berserker stole the well water before befouling it with the squirrel's blood. You are wasting your time in Vanaheimr."

"Where in Miðgarðr can I find Angantýr?" Skuld asked.

Evyndr replied with his eyes still closed, "He and his Berserker brothers sail for Samsø. That is where you will find and defeat him."

"Defeat?" Skuld questioned. "Am I not to bring him back to the well? He must reverse what he has done."

Evyndr tilted his head again and his brow furrowed. "Something is happening," he announced, full of concern. "The spirit of Fate has departed."

Skuld's brow puckered at the abrupt end. She couldn't tell if this magic had been impacted by Yggdrasil's sickness.

She held her head high. "It's no matter. We have the direction needed."

"You aren't really believing this, are you?" Brynhildr whispered as Freyja and Evyndr spoke quietly to each other.

Skuld downed the rest of her mead, allowing the thick liquid to slide around her tongue and down her throat effortlessly. "We need to gather our things and depart at once. It is a long way to Miðgarðr and we don't have enough time if Angantýr is sailing there now."

Brynhildr grabbed Skuld's arm and whirled her around so she could face her. "Do you hear yourself right now? You said yourself: even you, the Norn of what ought to be, had never even heard of this ritual before. My friend, I fear you are bewitched. I don't think we should trust these people."

Skuld removed her arm from Brynhildr's grasp. "I am not bewitched. Whatever spoke through Evyndr told the truth."

"What makes you so sure?"

She took hold of Brynhildr's hands and squeezed them as though she could impart the reason for her belief through mere touch alone. The answer tumbled out of Skuld's lips like a confession. "Because not once have I uttered Ratatǫskr's name anywhere in the Nine Realms. No one else knows he's dead." Skuld's eyes met Brynhildr's in a silent plea to accept and pursue the leads which had been revealed.

Brynhildr bit her lip against the misgivings she still harbored. Quietly, she said, "I know you want to believe this, but I have to tell you this doesn't feel right, Skuld."

Freyja interrupted their conversation by approaching and settling her arms over the two women's shoulders. "It seems you will be on your way to Miðgarðr then. I will have my servants provision you for your journey."

Brynhildr looked at the ground.

Skuld asked, "What is the fastest route?"

The goddess tapped her lips with a peeling finger. "That would be the Bifrǫst Bridge in Ásgarðr. It's the most direct route. Unfortunately, diplomatic relations being what they are, we cannot get you there."

"Then it should be obvious what they require," Evyndr spoke up. "They need your falcon skin."

The mention of her feathered cloak brought an odd flush to Freyja's cheeks. "My falcon skin? I hardly think that will work. Only one can wear it, and both must go."

Evyndr gave his mistress a long, hard stare. "You forget Brynhildr is a Valkyrie. She has her swan skin."

Freyja made a face before flouncing around. "Alright," she agreed testily. "Norn, you may borrow my falcon skin. I ask that, should our paths cross again, you return it to me, for it is a precious treasure and I loathe to part with."

Skuld gave a solemn nod. "I swear."

Without acknowledging Skuld's promise, Freyja left the main room into one of the smaller side rooms.

Evyndr handed Brynhildr her pack. "Here, don't forget this."

Hesitant and distrusting, the Valkyrie accepted her bag from the man. Her reaction made him smile more.

"I forget how judgmental the Æsir and their pets can be," he said.

This earned him a snarl from Brynhildr and he laughed. "Safe travels, Valkyrie."

At that moment, Freyja returned to the room carrying a cloak of brown falcon feathers. She dumped it into Skuld's arms. "You should both leave. You do not want to miss Angantýr."

"Yes. Thank you for your hospitality."

Evyndr watched Skuld as she called for Strix. His attention made her nervous and hyper-aware of every motion she made. The odd energy surrounding him seemed amplified. With her intuition screaming, she unfurled the feathered cloak in front of her. Inconspicuously withdrawing her dagger, she etched the runes for Evyndr's fate in the air between her and the barrier of the falcon skin.

A scattering of out-of-focus images appeared in her mind; blurred and indistinct. The strange smear of colors didn't feel like what ought to be. Instead, it had the stale, brittle feel of what once was. There was no future for the man before her and there hadn't been for a long time. Was this some effect of the dying tree? Were her powers leaving her? The very idea made her tremble.

With her mind full of troubling thoughts, Skuld walked out of Freyja's hall with Brynhildr at her side and Strix on her shoulder.

They traveled in pensive silence, each thinking about their encounter with Freyja.

Tired of the quiet, Brynhildr asked, "Do you believe everything Evyndr said during the Seiðr?"

Skuld sighed. "Yes, I do. I was skeptical at first, but he said Ratatoskr's name. I have not mentioned the name of Týrfingr's victim since I came to the realms. Evyndr couldn't have known."

Brynhildr blew out a long breath of air. "And according to Evyndr, the person who murdered is Angantýr. A human Berserker?"

"Yes, that is what Evyndr said."

Brynhildr frowned. "That doesn't seem right."

"Why not?" Skuld gave a sidelong glance to her friend.

"How could a human Berserker find a way to the base of Yggdrasil? Furthermore, if a Berserker killed the squirrel, then most of Miðgarðr would have heard about it by now. A feat like stealing water from the Well of Destiny is something a Berserker would brag about. They are not the most subtle of warriors. In fact, they would tell the tale as much as possible to increase their renown. If Miðgarðr had been told, then the gods would certainly know about it. So far, no one has said anything except for Evyndr and Freyja." Brynhildr's brow furrowed in thought.

Skuld pursed her lips. She hadn't considered this aspect, much less for Brynhildr to have such insight into the ways of the Nine Realms.

Taking Skuld's pensive silence as disbelief, Brynhildr shrugged. "All I am saying is things aren't adding up."

"You're right, they are not. Angantýr is still our best lead though. We have to follow it."

Halting at the edge of a field of tall grass, Brynhildr suggested, "Let's put the suits on over here."

After walking a few feet into the golden field of wild wheat, they came to a small spring that pooled into a calm stream. There by the bubbling waters, Brynhildr and Skuld donned the feather suits. Both the swan and falcon skins had been fashioned into cloaks with a metal circlet and pin to clasp it around their shoulders. Magic seeped out of the edges

As Skuld donned the falcon skin and clasped it around her neck, a strange, warm tingling sensation crept along her skin. The heat sunk deeper, penetrating her very bones as it grew hotter. Just when she thought she'd burst into flames if she didn't take it off, the heat stabilized, and then came the popping and shifting of her bones.

There was no pain; just a mild discomfort as her body morphed into that of a giant brown falcon. Her nose lengthened and hooked into a beak. Her eyes slanted to the sides even as her forehead narrowed. The sensation of her hair transforming into feathers felt like the tiny pinpricks of needles. The feet that helped her stand upright morphed into talons and the inequity of her weight distribution in her new body made Skuld stumble.

"Careful," Brynhildr honked at her. "Use your wings to balance."

As Skuld transformed into the falcon body Freyja's feather suit allowed, Brynhildr underwent her own transformation. Where the young Valkyrie should have been stood a tall, majestic swan.

"What magic makes this possible?" Skuld screeched, astonished. She stumbled over to the pool of water and peered at her reflection. A rather startled looking falcon with golden eyes and a black-tipped beak stared back. Her feathers were a nutmeg brown with sand-colored speckles.

"It's the magic of the suit," Brynhildr explained, still with the nasal honking quality to her speech. "All of the Valkyries have them. I've never seen a falcon one before though. Still, it is lucky we have it. Now we can fly to Ásgarðr and get to the Bifrǫst."

Skuld glanced over at Strix who watched all of this with a certain aloofness. He hooted as though telling them how silly they looked in feathers.

Skuld shifted from one foot to the other, minding the sharp, piercing talons at the edges. Her connection to the ground became strange and foreign. What Brynhildr explained made the Norn nervous. "So we can just fly? Instinctively?"

This point made the Swan-Valkyrie cock her head to the side as though she thought over the question. "You know, I am not precisely sure how it works. When I want to fly, I just think fly and my body does what it needs to. Must be the magic of the suit, I suppose."

"Just think fly?" Skuld repeated acerbically. "It is that simple, is it?"

"Use your instincts. It will be alright," Brynhildr assured her. To demonstrate, the Swan-Valkyrie leapt confidently into the air, spreading her massive white wings wide into the waiting sky. With strong, full beats of her wings, she rose higher and higher until she arced in a wide circle above the field where Skuld stood staring up at her.

The gracefulness and seeming simplicity of Brynhildr's take off quelled most of Skuld's doubts. Determined to try, she closed her golden falcon eyes, concentrated on what she imagined flying felt like, spread her wings, and leapt into the air.

She then promptly fell flat on her beak.

The sting of the impact with the ground didn't hurt as much as the loud honking laugh of Brynhildr the swan from above. In moments, the Valkyrie landed just as gracefully as she had taken off.

"You're thinking too much," Brynhildr admonished. "The key is not to think. Just do. Try again."

Skuld grudgingly got to her feet. If she had been in her usual form, her cheeks would have been crimson with embarrassment. Still, she would not be shown up by a Valkyrie. If Brynhildr could fly with such ease, then so could she.

It took a lot longer than Skuld would have liked, but, under the young Valkyrie's careful tutelage, she learned how to fly.

After practicing taking off and landing and a few mid-air maneuvers, Brynhildr pronounced Skuld ready for the trip to Ásgarðr. "You'll have to tell me when you get tired," she said as they prepared to take off. "It's easy to not notice and then the exhaustion will hit you hard. We will pace ourselves."

The urgency of needing to get to Miðgarðr as soon as possible warred with Brynhildr's advice. Reluctantly, Skuld agreed, "We go slow and steady."

She leapt into the air once more, pumping her wings perhaps not as gracefully as Brynhildr, but just as effective. Flying was an incredible feeling, once Skuld got used to it. The feel of the wind in her feathers and the moist clouds rushing past exhilarated her. Brynhildr shouted and performed daring loops that impressed Skuld.

"Come on! Give it a try!" the Valkyrie called out. "This is the most fun you'll ever have!"

Tentatively, the Norn tried a small, wobbly loop. Blood rushed to her head and the sudden disorientation made her gasp. When she righted herself, she found her breath came in quick soft pulsing exhales.

"That was amazing!" she cried out to the swan.

"I told you!"

Strix kept pace with the two women turned birds, albeit he flew steadier and without the dips and dives.

Skuld kept a watchful eye on the ground to keep track of where they were. The landscape shifted from green to brown and then to the light blue of the harbor which deepened to the darker, more primal indigo of the ocean.

"Don't head out over the water," Brynhildr warned.

"It's too windy and dangerous. We can keep to the coastline in case we need to land."

Even this close to the water the winds changed. They blew colder and with more force. The very air seemed wilder.

They settled into a steady rhythm. Time meant nothing up in the air. The connection with the sky was too great and Skuld could have been flying for minutes or hours, there was no way to tell. All she knew is she felt completely free.

Chapter Eight: Ásgarðr

They followed the jagged coastline, watching for the autumn covered shores of Ásgarðr. It wasn't long before they found the Ífingr River with one bank covered in the snows of mid-winter and the other set ablaze with the autumn leaves. They followed the river for a time before catching the updrafts of wind off of the mountains.

Skuld began to wonder where in Ásgarðr the Bifrǫst would be when something whizzed by her beak. Reacting to the abrupt projectile, she faltered in flight and reared backward. As she struggled to right herself and adjust course, another sharp object came flying at her and impaled itself into her wing.

Shock swiftly turned to pain which bled into rage. She screeched out her anger and hurt. Any movement she made with her wing caused terrible pain. Unable to continue flying, she tumbled out of the sky.

Brynhildr rushed to catch up with Skuld's descent, helpless to stop it. "Hold on!" she called out.

Skuld didn't hear her. Instead, she focused on the rapidly approaching ground and braced for impact.

The earth opened its arms to embrace Skuld as she plummeted from flight. Her falcon body met first with the trees, snapping the branches while gathering twigs and leaves with her descent. It happened so fast; for a brief moment, her mind wandered back to climbing the great Yggdrasil all the way to the top-most branches and looking down on all nine realms.

The branches grew thicker and thicker and their impacts had the unintended effect of slowing her descent. When she did hit the ground, it knocked her breath out of her and replaced all of her senses with nothingness.

Two figures peered over at her when she roused back to consciousness. The brightness of the sky eclipsed their features into shadowy blurs.

"I told you, Iðunn," one of the figures said. The voice sounded male to Skuld. "A fine prize for someone with my skills. This will feed us for the rest of our journey and then some."

"Don't be so sure," a woman, presumably Iðunn, responded. "Look, the poor bird is still alive."

Skuld heard the sound of a blade scraping against leather. "I can make quick work of that," the male said. "Perhaps we can roast it with some of your apples tonight."

Through the haze of pain, Skuld realized they meant to kill her, but she couldn't move or do anything to protect herself. She blinked frantically trying to get her mind to clear and to take some sort of action. She twitched one of her wings. A terrible, stinging flash of pain from her shoulder to the tip of her wing accompanied the movement. She cursed herself for ever learning how to fly.

"Wait!" Brynhildr shouted. She sounded so far away. Skuld craned her neck to see.

A flurry of white and brown feathers and a flash of talons overtook her vision as Strix flew in and attacked Skuld's would-be murderers.

The male's confused cries and the female's terrified screams filled the air. The furious flap of feathered wings and Strix's shriek gave Skuld the chance to roll over to the side that wasn't injured in an attempt to stand up.

Behind her were the supporting arms of Brynhildr, back in her human form. She did her best to get Skuld back to her feet as she gave a whispered plea, "Are you alright? Skuld, I thought you were dead!"

A loud, pain-filled screech made both of them turn towards the chaos Strix initiated. The small owl fell to the ground, a section of his white feathers bright with fresh blood.

The sight filled Skuld with dread and fury. Ignoring the pain in her left wing, she charged at the man standing over her oldest companion with murder in her eyes.

"Stop!" Brynhildr yelled. "Everyone calm down right now!"

The man held his knife out, ready to stab anyone else who came close. Stix lay on the ground, giving out a small pitiful cooing.

"Who are you?" the woman asked from behind the man.

"Why are you trying to make off with our dinner?" he demanded.

Brynhildr countered their questions with one of her own, "Why did you shoot my friend?"

"Friend? This is your friend? Do you consort exclusively with birds?"

Brynhildr's features took on a hard, angry cast. She reached to where the falcon feathered suit fastened together and undid the clasp.

Because of the arrow still embedded in her, the transformation back into her original form became agonizing. Skuld bore the pain in silence, her eyes locked on the still form of Strix a mere five feet ahead of where she stood. As soon as she completed the change, she wrenched herself out of Brynhildr's grasp and rushed to where Strix lay.

The abrupt transformation of their intended dinner into a young woman caused Iðunn to step backward and her hands to fly to her mouth in astonishment. "Loki, what have you done?" she whispered, horrified.

Loki, for his part, appeared no less shocked, but he

soon recovered himself. His face bled from the sharp taloned attack the owl had launched at him.

"Who are you?" he demanded. "What sorcery is this?"

Skuld ignored him and cradled Strix in her arms. He still lived, but the wound was grave. He hooted softly as Skuld got to her feet, clasping him against her breast. Her fingers traced the blood coating his feathers.

"I am one of Óðinn's Valkyries," Brynhildr stated as haughtily as she could. "And I recognize you, Loki Laufeyson. I should not be surprised by your behavior. I've heard many stories of your mischief."

Not liking being challenged in such an insolent way, the thin, wild-haired god turned to Brynhildr, his dagger still drawn and malice in his movements. "Careful, girl," he warned. His black eyes glittered with danger.

Faced with an open threat from a god, Brynhildr lifted her chin defiantly, though with a perceptible tremble in her limbs and a faltering of her stance. For the first time, Skuld detected the presence of fear in the young woman.

"Please," Iðunn said speaking up, "We do not wish to quarrel."

"Then why did you attack us?" Brynhildr demanded.

The goddess demurred, casting her gaze down. "Loki was hunting for our dinner. We did not know his prey were not really birds. Surely you can understand that."

"Indeed, it seems you've cheated me out of my quarry. You owe me recompense. Give me the owl and we will part as friends," Loki spoke up. "It is not long until it is dead now anyway. Then what use is it to you?"

With murder in her eyes, Skuld regarded the lanky man and the golden, delicate female before her. She ignored the wound in her shoulder and stood up to her full height. Her rage knew no bounds. She wanted to kill them. She had the will to carve the two offenders to pieces and let the ravens eat their fill from the corpses.

However, she recognized both of them. Loki and Iðunn played integral parts for Ragnarǫk. She could not just kill them outright.

Skuld transferred Strix to Brynhildr, hissing at the sting when she moved her injured arm.

Pulling her mind away from such violent fantasies, Skuld gazed down at Strix, her oldest friend. Just above his wound, she gently etched a healing rune. The sigil flickered with power, but faded all too quickly. "No," she whispered, desperate to stop everything if she could just save her friend.

"I can help," Iðunn offered. "I know how to stitch up some wounds and some minor healing magic."

When neither Skuld nor Brynhildr declined her offer, Iðunn made her way to them.

"He's in pain. I don't know if I can heal these wounds. My runes . . . they are not working."

Iðunn thought she could detect the hint of helplessness in the young woman's voice. "Let me try," the goddess suggested. "Sometimes healing is best done by someone that is not so invested in the outcome."

Skuld gave her a funny look as the goddess reached in and inspected the owl's wounds.

Brynhildr held steadfastly to Strix, unwilling to hand him over to one of the people who wanted to eat him. Her hand strayed to the hilt of her sword.

"Hold him here," she told Brynhildr, positioning the Valkyrie's hands away from her weapon and on the owl to stop the blood flow. "There's one major wound here, but it is in such a place that it's hard to get to. The best thing I can do is clean it and try and staunch the bleeding. Only time will tell if it can be healed. Unless you can heal him with your magic?" Iðunn glanced over at Skuld in askance.

She bowed her head, wincing as her wound reacted to her movement. "I cannot. I tried."

"Try again, please. I think it may just be the shock

that's preventing you."

Giving a tiny nod of agreement, Skuld held out her hands tracing healing runes above Strix and put as much love and power behind it as possible.

As she did, Iðunn reached into one of the pouches that lined her belt and withdrew a small wad of moss. She wiped at the wound, removing the excess blood to better see the cut.

As Skuld whispered the runes and traced them in the air, the cut in the bird's flesh sealed itself closed. The whispering stopped and Skuld's hand fell to her side with a throbbing gasp.

Strix lay still in Brynhildr's arms. Iðunn leaned in and watched the owl's chest, waiting for the telltale breaths that would indicate if he still lived. There were none.

The goddess turned a sorrowful glance at the young woman who watched her companion with tears threatening to fall from her eyes.

"Strix," Skuld whispered as her face crumpled in pain and grief.

Iðunn stepped back, allowing Brynhildr to comfort her companion.

"Skuld, I am so sorry," the Valkyrie said. "I am so sorry."

Loki gave a chuckle as he leaned against a thick tree. "Well, ladies. Shall I start preparing our meal?"

The question and the mocking tone reignited Skuld's rage. Fueled by fresh grief, it burned hotter than before.

Noticing Skuld's barely restrained boiling anger, Loki laughed. "Surely you are not so attached to the thing as to deny hungry people the food they rightfully killed? Come, we will be gracious hosts and allow you to dine with us before you go along your way and we ours."

Brynhildr held her breath, waiting to see what Skuld would do in the face of such an outrageous suggestion.

Skuld reached for her obsidian dagger, hefting it into

the palm of her right hand, considering its weight and how nice it would look with the blade between the insolent god's eyes.

"Loki Laufeyson, you do not want this fight," she intoned.

The god spread his arms out wide. "There is no fight here. I demand my kill and you may go."

There would be no reasoning with him. That suited Skuld just fine. Still, regardless of her feelings, regardless of the pleasure she would take from killing him as payment for Strix's life, she could not. Loki served a grander purpose in the events to come.

But that did not mean she couldn't maim him.

Her fury overrode the doubt of her powers. With all of her rage focused into the dagger, she drew the runes between her and Loki.

The sigils lit up the air between them with an otherworldly golden glow. Sparks flew out of the tip of her dagger as she poured her hate into the runes.

When she finished with her incantation, Loki's mouth disappeared, leaving a strange swath of skin in its place.

"I would kill you without a second thought. I could do it too, in a million ways over a million lifetimes. My sisters and I would uncarve the very thought of you from the realms to pay for what you have done. Great suffering is coming your way, Loki Laufeyson. There is nothing you can do to stop it."

Runes flashed in her eyes. She stared straight into Loki's soul, imparting everything she knew of what destiny had in store for the trickster.

Loki stared back, unable to look away. In his mind, he saw visions and experienced echoes of the agony yet to come. His arms were stiff at his side as though he had been bound by a rope so tightly there wasn't even room for him to struggle against it.

When all of the misery had been shown, Skuld

decided, "I will allow you to have your voice back but know what you have seen cannot be undone. Your fate is fixed."

Loki trembled at her declaration.

Skuld returned her dagger to its sheath. She approached the frozen god who watched her every move. Sweat broke out on his pale brow, plastering strands of dark hair to his face in thread-like wisps.

Skuld took Loki's dagger from his hands, noticing the bright red blood glistening on its edges. The sight caused a fresh wave of fury to wash over her. Strix's blood. Riding the emotion, she brought the dagger up to Loki's face and savagely sawed the blade into the skin just below his hooked nose where his mouth should be.

Loki's blood spilled as she carved a mouth where she had taken his own. She purposefully made the opening crooked and edges wider than they would have been naturally out of spite. When she finished, she returned the dagger to the god. "There. You have your voice back."

The god staggered backward away from the Norn, his hands reaching up to inspect the wound. When he drew his fingers away, they were soaked in his blood.

Loki gave a final, horrified look at Skuld before darting into the woods. Before long a wounded, sustained howl filled the air.

Skuld returned to where Brynhildr held Strix.

Her rage spent, only a deep, unyielding grief remained. Strix had been her companion for many cycles. He had been her best friend; the one she could talk to besides her sisters. The one who accompanied her on her carving tasks up and down the trunk of the great Yggdrasil. The one who foraged with her, who gazed up at the swirling galaxies in the never-ending expanse of sky above the top-most branches.

Skuld couldn't look at Strix's body, so she turned away, her head in her hands and tears spilling from her eyes. Never before did she feel such crushing pain or sorrow. Never before had death become so personal. Sure Ratatǫskr's death had been a shock, but he had not been as close to her as Strix. Strix was family.

With her head hanging low, Brynhildr respectfully set Strix's lifeless body on a nearby rock. As she did, his wings fell open as though he were soaring high overhead.

The Valkyrie went to Skuld and, using her sternest voice said, "Come here, Skuld. We need to get that arrow out of you."

Iðunn watched as the grieving woman submitted to the younger's ministrations.

"Well? Are you going to help or not?" Brynhildr called out to the goddess.

Startled at being called out, Iðunn blinked. "Me?"

"Who else is here? I need help. I can't hold her and remove the arrow on my own."

The goddess rushed forward, her mind snapping back to the healing needing to be done. Together, she and the Valkyrie held the weeping Skuld down and extracted Loki's arrow from her shoulder. They dressed her wound and, when it was all over, they sat in awkward silence, unsure of what to say.

At last, Brynhildr offered her hand to Iðunn. "Thank you for your help. I am Brynhildr."

Accepting the offer of friendship, the goddess grasped the Valkyrie's hand. "I am Iðunn, Keeper of the Apples of Immortality."

Brynhildr's eyebrows rose betraying her interest. "Why were you traveling with Loki?"

"I wasn't. We happened to meet earlier today as I made my way to Himinbjǫrg. It is customary for me to offer a sample of this year's crop to Heimdallr. Loki sought to woo me with his hunting skills. His boasting is what led to this unfortunate accident."

To Skuld, those last words *unfortunate accident* thudded in the chasm of her chest where her grief pooled. She sat with her pain, growing accustomed to its weight and wondering how long she would have to carry it forward. She wondered if she were strong enough to handle such a burden. How did these mortals do it so often?

Brynhildr seized upon a different part of Iðunn's explanation. "You are going to see Heimdallr? We were traveling to the Bifrǫst. We have business in Miðgarðr we need to attend right away."

"It's not far from here, maybe half a days' journey if we walk."

The Valkyrie glanced at Skuld and the makeshift bandages adorning her shoulder. "It seems walking is the best way since we can no longer fly."

"What about Strix?" Skuld asked, surprising the two women. She had been so caught up in her grief that neither Brynhildr nor Iðunn expected her to come out of it for quite some time.

"What should we do with his body?" Skuld clarified when neither of the women answered.

Brynhildr glanced at where she left the owl; his back against the boulder and his wings wide open to receive the blessing of the sun and the sky. His feet and talons curled as though they held a mouse. "We should bury him," she decided. "He deserves the honor of a proper burial."

Skuld looked at the Valkyrie with a mixture of confusion and gratefulness. "How does one honor a dead family member? I've orchestrated death, but this is different. I don't want to do the wrong thing."

Brynhildr couldn't help but comfort Skuld with an embrace. "He died fighting, so he is not without honor. We will bury him here, where he can see the sky. If it is alright with you, I will prepare him."

The thoughtfulness in Brynhildr's answer brought a fresh onslaught of tears to the Norn. Unable to speak, she nodded and wiped at the dampness sliding down her cheeks.

Brynhildr went to pick up the owl's body. "Iðunn, would you please assist me?" she asked as she gestured with her head towards the edge of the woods.

Iðunn cast a worried glance at Skuld as she stood. "Will you be alright?"

Numbly, Skuld nodded. She watched the goddess and the Valkyrie confer over Strix's body as they disappeared beyond the tree line.

Skuld doubted she would feel better after they buried her friend. It was just a body, after all. What made Strix was no longer there. The husk left behind was just that; a husk.

"I should have killed Loki," she muttered to herself as she hugged her knees to her chest. Her shoulder twinged, but the pain could not compare to the ache throbbing in her heart.

Before long, both Iðunn and Brynhildr returned carrying the small body of the owl wrapped in Brynhildr's cloak. The sight of the bundle brought a lump to Skuld's throat.

"Would you like to hold him while I dig the grave?" Brynhildr asked her friend. "So you can say goodbye?"

Trembling and once again on the verge of tears, Skuld nodded. Brynhildr placed the wrapped bundle into Skuld's arms.

She hugged it to her chest, not wanting to let him go. She wished she'd stayed at home with her sisters; that she'd simply allowed whatever end to come. In her mind, she cursed Loki and she cursed Freyja, she cursed the murderer of Ratatoskr, and she cursed her sisters for letting her go on such a futile mission. If not for this fool's errand, Strix would still be alive.

All too soon Brynhildr approached her. "It's time."

Skuld struggled to her feet, accepting Brynhildr's steadying hand. Together they walked to a small open trench next to a pile of stones.

"What do I do?" Skuld asked the Valkyrie.

Brynhildr gently guided her friend through the motions. "Put him in the grave and then say goodbye."

Hesitantly, Skuld as she was told. She didn't want to let Strix go. She lingered over the hole, taking her time to set Strix in just right and to securely tighten the knots on the bundle so they wouldn't come loose.

Finally satisfied with his placement, Skuld rose to her feet.

Brynhildr stood next to her and offered her hand as the Norn began to speak.

Clutching Brynhildr's hand, Skuld spoke, her voice breaking with her sorrow. "Strix was more than a friend; he was my family. His spirit soared above all others. Fate decreed his journey to come to an end. I will miss him."

The words did little to quench Skuld's grief, but she was glad she got to say them.

Together, they began placing stones atop of Strix's wrapped body.

When the final stone had been set, the sun had sunk behind the hills.

"Let us leave," Skuld said. Her emotions were chaotic inside her mind and she had no desire to linger within sight of the burial mound.

"But it is dark now," Iðunn protested. "Wouldn't it be better to wait through the night and depart at dawn?"

Brynhildr shrugged at Skuld. "She has a point. Traveling through the forest is more dangerous in the dark."

Skuld shook her head. "No, we have to get to Samsø. I must intercept Angantýr."

"Why? I don't understand why it is so urgent for you to get to Miðgarðr that you cannot even pause for a night." Iðunn's confusion slowed her movements.

Skuld regarded the goddess coldly. "Our business is none of yours. You can come with us or you can stay. I take no responsibility for you."

Shock and hurt crossed over Iðunn's delicate

features. A flush of anger rose to her cheeks. "You ungrateful wretch!"

"Hold on!" Brynhildr interjected before the situation could spiral out of control. "Iðunn, there are things you don't understand and it's better if you don't. Skuld and I are on an important quest. Already we are delayed because of Loki and the death of our dear owl companion. If you choose not to accompany us, then please point us in the right direction of where Himinbjǫrg is. We aim to meet Heimdallr and travel the Bifrǫst into Miðgarðr before dawn."

Iðunn flicked her gaze between Brynhildr and Skuld, trying to discern what context she missed. "Alright, I will take you to the home of Heimdallr. He is already expecting me," she said at last. As she shouldered her pack, she gestured to a partially hidden path off to the left. "This way. It's a good thing the moon is full tonight. Otherwise, we would be lost."

Together they set off down the path towards the home of the whitest of gods, Heimdallr.

Skuld found the movement and the dedication to her purpose didn't lessen her sorrow for Strix. She felt it with every breath and every step she took. This reaction, this prolonged suffering was completely new to her. Again, she marveled at the stamina of humans and gods alike who dealt with this pain continuously.

The three unlikely traveling companions arrived at Heimdallr's home late into the night, and well before dawn broke. The hall known as Himinbjǫrg stood tall against the mountain boundaries of Ásgarðr. The rainbow colors of the Bifrǫst burned just beyond the great hall, illuminating the glade of the spacious home as bright as day. Thick, luscious grass blanketed the field, a stark contrast to the rough, rocky mountainside trail they traveled for most of their journey.

The sight of the bright hall brought a sigh of relief from Iðunn. "Heimdallr is waiting for us. I am sure he knows we are close."

"How can you tell?" Brynhildr asked as she gazed in wonder at the Bifrǫst. "We've only just gotten through the trees."

"Heimdallr can see the worlds and hear the grass grow. He's probably known for some time we are drawing nearer," Iðunn explained.

The Keeper of the Apples was right. As they approached the hall, a tall, muscular god with a thick beard emerged from a thick door.

"Welcome!" he bellowed and spread his arms wide to receive his guests. "Iðunn, I have missed you. Who is it you bring to my doorstep?"

"I've brought two who seek to cross the Bifrǫst," Iðunn called as she strode closer to the hall. "They have urgent business in the land of men."

Heimdallr lowered his arms. "Is that so? Come forward, friends of Iðunn. Let me gaze upon your faces."

Brynhildr and Skuld glanced at each other before they followed Iðunn to the steps of the hall.

Heimdallr met Iðunn with a familiar embrace and a large smile. "It has been a long time, my friend. I hope your travels have been kind."

Iðunn returned the smile. "Indeed, it has been a journey I am not likely to forget any time soon. Things are very strange in Ásgarðr. Once these two are on their way, we shall have a glass of mead and I will tell you about it."

Curious, the god cocked his head to the side but accepted her deferment.

He turned to Brynhildr next, the radiant smile still bright and welcoming. "A Valkyrie! Brynhildr, if I am not mistaken?"

Surprised, Brynhildr stammered, "Uh, yes. I am Brynhildr. How did you know?"

Heimdallr laughed. "It is my business to know a great many things. One of which is to know who Óðinn has conscripted into his service. I must say, you have quite the reputation, even among his Choosers of the Slain."

The acknowledgement made Brynhildr blush with pride.

Heimdallr turned then to Skuld. Swiftly he bowed his head. "My lady, it is an honor to welcome you to Himinbjǫrg. How may I serve you?"

Heimdallr's reaction to Skuld made Iðunn frown. "Why do you honor her so?" she asked her friend. "She's naught but a Valkyrie's companion."

The ignorance Iðunn showed scandalized Heimdallr. He whirled around to face the Keeper of the Apples. "Are you blind? Can you not see this is one of the three Nornir whose sacred duty it is to care for the great ash tree, Yggdrasil?"

Heimdallr's revelation made Iðunn's sun-kissed face lighten by three shades. "Is it so?" she asked meekly, staring at Skuld for confirmation.

Brynhildr answered for the Norn, smug as only the young can be. "I told you there's much you didn't understand, Iðunn."

Heimdallr ignored both Brynhildr and Iðunn, turning his full attention on Skuld. Noticing her red, puffy eyes, fresh from crying tears of sorrow and the way she favored her left arm, he inquired, "What has happened, my lady? How did you come to be wounded and why are you so full of sorrow?"

The sudden attention and hospitableness of an Æsir set Skuld on edge. She'd had nothing but trouble from everyone she'd met in the realms and she was hesitant to trust yet another. Besides, she did not have the time to explain herself to this watchman of Ásgarðr. Enough time had been wasted.

"Brynhildr and I must cross the Bifrǫst. There is important work we must do in Miðgarðr."

Heimdallr brought his hand to his chin and ran his

fingers through his beard. For a moment, Skuld thought he would delay them even further by refusing to allow her and Brynhildr to pass until he had the story out of them. However, the god surprised her. He asked, "Where in Miðgarðr will your journey take you?"

"The island of Samsø," Skuld answered. "There is someone there I must meet."

The watchman of the gods gave a single, grave nod. "Come with me."

He marched down the steps of his hall and headed towards the Bifrǫst. Skuld and Brynhildr followed in his wake while Iðunn trailed further behind.

The Bifrǫst burned before them, a rainbow of light and mist which served as a pathway between Ásgarðr and Miðgarðr. The bright colors flickered like a flame. The four came to the beginning or, depending on one's point of view, the end of the Bifrǫst. Heimdallr reached out and waved his hands in the shimmering light, making adjustments to something neither Skuld nor Brynhildr could see.

"There have been malfunctions recently. The Bifrǫst has not guided travelers accurately. I know not what causes it, but should you find yourself somewhere other than you intended, call my name. I will hear you and work to get you back."

His admission solidified the growing fear in Skuld's heart. The realms were breaking apart. How much time did Yggdrasil have left?

Refusing to dwell on the question, Skuld regarded the bridge and out of curiosity extended her hand into the mass of colors. The colors dancing like flames were warm mist against her skin.

"It is ready, my lady," Heimdallr said, removing his hands from the colored mist. "Do you require anything more for your journey?"

Brynhildr glanced at Skuld. The Norn answered, "No. Thank you, Heimdallr. Your assistance and haste will be remembered."

Heimdallr gave a final courteous bow. "I will keep watch for you, my lady."

"Wait," Brynhildr spoke up. "What are we supposed to do?"

"Walk into the Bifrǫst. When you emerge, you will be where you needed to be. Stay within the colors until you get there. If you don't, then you will fall off of the bridge and be stuck between the worlds."

The young Valkyrie gulped and grabbed for Skuld's hand. She allowed Brynhildr to take it, though secretly she was grateful to have the firm grip clasping tight.

"Safe travels," Heimdallr said. Iðunn waved in the background, still in awe and surprised by the identity of her traveling companion.

Together, Skuld and Brynhildr immersed themselves in the shimmering warm colors of the Bifrǫst. They could only see a few feet ahead of them. Anything beyond remained shrouded by the mist. Brynhildr kept a firm grip on Skuld's hand, not wanting to stray too far off course. They pressed forward, determined to make it to Samsø.

When it seemed they had been walking for hours, Skuld glanced over at the Valkyrie. "I never said thank you."

"What?"

"I never thanked you for what you did back there with Loki and Iðunn. And how you handled Strix's . . ." the mere mention of her beloved owl's name made her choke up. "Thank you for all of that."

Surprised at the sudden outpouring of emotion, Brynhildr squeezed Skuld's hand.

Skuld coughed, taking a minute to clear the tears from her eyes. "I know I am not the easiest person to get along with. I truly didn't expect that interacting with the people in the realms to be so difficult. I want to let you know even though we fight, I do appreciate everything you've done for me since we've met."

Brynhildr smiled at her. "You are welcome. That is what friends are supposed to do." Knowing better than to press Skuld any farther or to let her dwell too much, she changed the subject. "If someone were to get ahold of the water from the Well of Destiny, what would happen?"

Skuld composed herself and focused on what Brynhildr asked. "Similar to drinking from the Well of Wisdom, if one drinks from the Well of Destiny, they would be able to change their fate. They would be able to deviate from the path the runes had carved for them."

"That's if they drink the water?" Brynhildr asked.

"Yes."

The colored mists of the Bifrǫst disappeared, leaving Skuld and Brynhildr atop a hill in a dark, wooded area. Below, the trees tapered off to give way to a small beach where a ship was moored. Voices shouted in the distance.

Brynhildr grabbed Skuld and pulled her behind a tree and hefted her sword in her hand.

Before either could make a move, the voices faded away. Brynhildr did not sheathe her sword, however, her arm trembled showing her fear.

"Angantýr must be close," Skuld whispered as she removed herself from behind the tree.

A beacon of green light lit up the darkened sky, coloring the moonlight in a sickly tinge. The sight halted both women in their tracks. The glow emanated from further up the hill.

Cries of fear came from the ships. "The barrows," the men muttered amongst themselves. "This island is for the dead. We should leave."

"What of Hjǫrvard? Would we just leave him?"

"He's the only one foolish enough to explore a haunted island by the moonlight. He is in Fate's hands now. I will not die by the hand of Angantýr's ghost!"

The sentiment was shared by several of the men. Within moments, the crew boarded the ship and headed out for the open ocean.

"Wait, Angantýr is dead?" Brynhildr asked. "I thought he was just getting here."

Skuld's features were hard as the realization settled over her. "It means we've been tricked."

Brynhildr glanced back, wondering at the harshness of her tone. In the dying light of the ghostly barrows, the young Valkyrie saw the glint of a sword and the momentary flash of a hooded figure behind Skuld.

Chapter Nine: Battle Cry

"Watch out!" she shouted and pushed Skuld out of the way of the attack. Both women fell to the ground, Brynhildr narrowly missing the edge of the blade. An odd humming emanated from inside the hooded cloak. Not quite a full melody, the notes were breathed more than sung, but the air changed.

The assailant grunted and swung again. The movements were clumsy and inexperienced as if the sword was too heavy and unbalanced for the person wielding it. Brynhildr hid her face as their attacker moved in for a closer range.

Skuld, however, kept her wits about her. She shrugged Brynhildr off of her and brought up Týrfingr to block the downswing of the attacker. She kicked at the enemy, her boot landing solidly in their groin. The humming ceased and the attacker let out a strangled cry as they fell back, allowing the tip of the sword to drag along the ground.

Skuld took the opportunity to get to her feet and drew her dagger. The hooded figure wasn't prepared for her magical attack. As the rune spell fizzled, its target stumbled back a few feet. Skuld cursed under her breath. She meant to send the assailant flying into the tree line.

Her heart skipped a beat when she realized Brynhildr remained on the ground. Had she been hurt? No time for her to check; the assailant rushed forward in another attack. Skuld swung her sword, miraculously connecting with the attacker's left arm.

The figure cried out in pain, clutching their wounded arm. Blood flowed freely onto the ground. Even wounded, the assailant didn't stop. They pitched forward in desperation, throwing their full weight into the Norn causing her to lose her grip on her sword and fall backward. The hood over the attacker's face flew back in the fight.

Skuld gasped at the sight of Evyndr. Shock made her freeze in place, her mind not quite comprehending what she saw.

The unmasking of the enemy brought Brynhildr to her feet. A gleam shone in her eyes and she rushed to attack.

Brynhildr raised her weapon, ready to strike when Evyndr began to sing an unfamiliar song. The effect, however, was immediate.

Abruptly, Brynhildr let out a pained cry as her sword clattered to the dirt. A moment later, the Valkyrie crumpled onto the ground, her hands over her ears and her eyes squeezed shut. She would not stop screaming.

Unsure of what happened, Skuld rushed to her companion. Fear pumped through her veins. "Brynhildr, stop!"

The screams didn't stop though. The gut-wrenching shrieks of terror were soul-shaking and teeth-rattling cries of help and hopelessness all at once.

Seizing the opportunity, Evyndr jumped to his feet and ran for the trees. Skuld wanted to follow, wanted to capture him, but hesitated to leave Brynhildr. In the end, she watched helplessly as the mysterious Vanir vanished in the night leaving a faint trail of blood drops which ended a few yards away.

Cursing her luck, Skuld did her best to check Brynhildr over for wounds. She wasn't injured or otherwise hurt. To get her to calm down, she grasped

Brynhildr's shoulders. "It's okay," she shouted, trying to be heard over the screams. "Brynhildr stop, you are alright."

The sound of Skuld's voice and the solid feel of her hands pinning her down centered Brynhildr. Her screams subsided and in time, she allowed her hands to fall away from her ears and she squinted her eyes open. Skuld knelt next to her, anger and overwhelming confusion making her face stern.

"What is wrong with you?" she demanded. "Why are you screaming?"

Trembling with fear, Brynhildr glanced around. Darkness reigned on the island. Even the ghost light from Angantýr's barrow had been extinguished.

"I — I heard him," the Valkyrie whispered. "He got into my head. I felt so hopeless. I couldn't fight. I couldn't do anything. Terrible things flashed in my mind. Skuld, I don't know how or why, but he's gotten into my head."

"Who?" Skuld demanded. "What did you see?"

"I don't know," Brynhildr wailed. "I can't know for sure. But Skuld, the terrible things he showed me. Corpses of everyone I know and love. The suffering before they were killed. The water, churning and wild, like a storm at sea. I can't stop it. I can't fight. If I do, terrible things will happen."

"What nonsense is this? Of course, you can fight. You are a Valkyrie, a Chooser of the Slain. You fight well, it is what you do. Now come on, get up. We have to get out of here. This was a trap." Skuld hid her concern at the way Brynhildr spoke. It sounded as though she'd seen a future of some kind, though not the same one Skuld saw before.

Her violent reaction made sense, though. Anyone untrained in the ways of the runes could be rendered a gibbering idiot if they were exposed to the reality of their fate. Knowledge of the future could be a dangerous thing in the hands of those not ready for it.

What concerned Skuld more was if the Valkyrie had

seen her future, then it had changed. That meant things were progressing in the wrong direction. Without knowing for certain, and with her powers weakened so much, Skuld felt helpless.

With these worries weighing on her, Skuld helped Brynhildr unsteadily to her feet. The eastern horizon lightened with the approaching dawn.

"What happened to my Valkyrie?" a deep, yet familiar voice asked.

Surprised, the two women turned to find an old man dressed in gray standing near them. One eye glittered with cunning intelligence from under the shadow created by his wide-brimmed hat.

Skuld stopped, her arms still around Brynhildr who laughed with wild relief even as her tears continued streaming down her cheeks.

"What do you want, One Eye?" Skuld asked.

The god eyed Skuld. "The battle draws near. I need my Valkyrie."

A despairing and frantic moan escaped Brynhildr's lips and she clawed at Skuld in terror. "No, please. I cannot fight. Do not make me fight!"

The desperate pleading took the god aback. "What is this? Why is my Brynhildr acting so cowardly?"

"I do not know. Something happened when she fought just now. She stopped and fell to the ground screaming."

Frowning, Óðinn squinted his good eye at his ward, searching for the difference within her. There was no wound he could detect. "She is fine," he said, confused. "She must come with me. The war with the Vanir has escalated. Battle calls."

Brynhildr burst into tears. "No! Please don't make me. Skuld, please! I can't do this. Terrible things will happen. Horrible things will come. I can't fight."

Upon hearing this, Óðinn's features darkened into a terrible scowl. "What nonsense is this? Enough, I tell you.

You will do your duties as a Valkyrie or so help me."

Not liking how the god treated Brynhildr, Skuld piped up, "She can't be left alone when she is so vulnerable."

"And who made her so vulnerable?" Óðinn wanted to know. "I think you are up to something, Norn. Did you do this to her? Did you use your magic to make her useless to me?"

Skuld snarled at the accusation. "Careful, One Eye."

Óðinn's scowl deepened. "I will take my Valkyrie and she will be cared for by her own kind."

Skuld glanced down at Brynhildr. The Valkyrie gazed back up at her, petrified tears welled in her bright blue eyes. She didn't speak, but her expression said everything Skuld needed to hear. The terror in Brynhildr's eyes cemented Skuld's decision. "I owe Brynhildr my life. She is my friend and I will not abandon her. I will go with her and I will join the fight against the Vanir."

The god stroked his gray beard, considering the implications of the Norn's offer.

"Alright then. We must journey to Valhǫll. The battle will begin soon and we must prepare." The god began walking purposefully towards the woods.

Skuld followed with Brynhildr shuffling next to her.

Brynhildr whispered to herself, "I can't fight. Please, don't make me fight."

Skuld frowned at her friend's babbling. Never would Brynhildr refuse to fight. Never had there been such a fearful streak evident in her before now.

Something changed the young woman. Something insidious. What could have shaken the Valkyrie's confidence so much to make her fear battle? It must have been some sort of spell. She hadn't seen any runes drawn though. A curse then? Curses could be etched into objects and easily placed near their victim.

Skuld's mind whirled, trying to understand. Then it dawned on her.

"Wait," the Norn demanded of Óðinn. She turned Brynhildr to face her and started inspecting her armor.

Confused and fearful, Brynhildr asked, "What are you doing?"

"Just trust me," Skuld said and continued her search.

Óðinn watched the exchange but didn't say anything.

At last, there was a sharp scrape against Skuld's fingers as she checked the lacings on the sides of Brynhildr's breastplate. She withdrew a bone fragment roughly half the size of her finger and just as wide. Warm to the touch, the power emanating from it was enough to make Skuld wonder how neither she nor Óðinn hadn't noticed it before.

Upon closer inspection, she noted several figures etched into the side. An incantation, but the script stopped her in her tracks. It was old, much older than this current cycle they were on. The runes had been written the same way as the runes on Týrfingr. Similar to how handwriting changed from person to person, the style of the runes appearance in each cycle changed ever so slightly. From what Skuld could tell, Týrfingr and this curse were from the same cycle.

"What is it?" Óðinn intoned as he peered over Skuld's shoulder.

Still puzzling over the implications of her discovery, she held the bone fragment aloft so the one-eyed god could examine it. "I believe this is the cause of Brynhildr's malady."

Óðinn took the piece of bone in his thick, weathered hands.

"My what?" Brynhildr asked, panic lacing her question. "What is it?"

After scrutinizing it, Óðinn let out a soft grunt and flung the piece of bone to the ground. Before Skuld could stop him, he smashed it with the end of his walking stick.

As the object shattered, Brynhildr let out a shriek before passing out.

"You fool!" Skuld yelled and dove for the unconscious Valkyrie. She still breathed, but Skuld worried the fall would have damaged her head.

"She will be fine. We must go before the bridge moves," Óðinn replied. He bent down and hoisted Brynhildr's limp body up with his strong arms and kept walking.

Skuld gathered Brynhildr's things before following after Óðinn. As she walked, shame overcame her. She'd been so gullible to trust the Vanir. Brynhildr was right all along not to trust Freyja and Evyndr. But how did they know about the death of Ratatoskr?

The answer sent chills down Skuld's spine. Either they knew the killer or they did the deed themselves. The whole trip to Miðgarðr and Samsø had been a trap designed to get Skuld off of their trail.

Why would they do such a thing? Why go through so much trouble to get Skuld out of the way? Why send her so far for a trap? It made more sense for them to kill her when she visited them. Why such a ruse to get her to Miðgarðr?

Consideration also needed to be given to the how. How did two Týrfingr's manage to exist in the same cycle? How did the Vanir manage to sneak into Skuld's home? The sisters laid out a special path for Óðinn when the time came for his sacrifice. No such path had been laid for the Vanir. Furthermore, how did she not see any of this in the runes she carved into Yggdrasil? No matter how she tried to understand, the puzzle pieces would not fit together.

Before long, the three travelers were back at the Bifrøst, its ever-swirling colors barely perceptible in the light of day. Óðinn gave the Norn a small nudge.

"After you," he said courteously though no warmth colored his words. His countenance projected grave seriousness.

Brynhildr remained unconscious and slung over the

god's shoulder. Worry permeated Skuld's features at the sight of her motionless friend. Brynhildr always suspected the events at Freyja's hall. She hadn't trusted them. Skuld should have listened to her instead of writing off her reaction as mere prejudice.

Shaking her head free of the mire of what could have been and from all of the questions with no answers, Skuld stepped forward into the rainbow mists and towards a battle that would bring her face to face with the enemies who always managed to elude her.

That evening, all of the Æsir gods arrived in Valhǫll for the customary feast the night before battle. The spirits of the human warriors the Valkyries plucked from Miðgarðr's battlefields eagerly basked in the glory the gods bestowed upon them. They would be ready to fight as Óðinn's army when the dawn came. Brynhildr's sisters in arms, the Valkyries, drank with gods and warriors alike, laughing and making merry amongst the candlelight.

Skuld watched all of this from a darkened corner of the hall, her plate of food untouched.

"Why aren't you joining the celebration?" a familiar voice inquired.

Skuld looked to see Brynhildr smiling down at her. Relief flooded through the Norn. "You are awake," she said as she motioned for her friend to sit with her. "The Valkyries were able to heal you after all. I worried you would miss the battle."

The Valkyrie laughed and slid onto the bench next to Skuld. "You know me. Nothing can keep me from fighting."

The comment froze Skuld's relieved smile. "What do you remember?"

Brynhildr bowed her head in shame. "Everything. I

know how I behaved and I know I have brought dishonor to my reputation by my cowardly actions. I hope to redeem myself in tomorrow's battle."

Skuld heaved a sigh and reached across the table to hold Brynhildr's hand. "You were under a curse. The actions were not yours. You could not help it."

The Valkyrie gave her a haunted look. "But the feeling. The fear it's still with me. It permeates my every thought. I would not wish this on my worst enemy, this terror at things one cannot control."

"Still, you are not so afraid of battle any longer, are you?" Skuld asked. Mentally she cursed Óðinn for breaking the charm in such a way. More care should have been given to its destruction. If she had time to study it, she may have been able to reverse it without the after-effects lingering in Brynhildr's mind.

"No, not quite. At least it is nothing I cannot quell." The young woman took a deep breath. "But that is not why I sought you out tonight. I did not intend to talk to you about my troubles."

Skuld raised an eyebrow at this proclamation. "What do you want to speak about?"

"This." The young Valkyrie presented a folded length of cloth by laying it on the table between them.

Skuld frowned. "What is this? I've no need for cloth."

Brynhildr laughed. "No, unwrap it. Your gift is inside."

"Gift?" Curiosity got the better of her as she unraveled the length of homespun material. Feathers lay pressed between the folds. The sight of the white plumes speckled with brown made Skuld freeze with the memory of Strix. Her breath caught in her throat. "What is this?" she choked out.

Unsure if the emotion being displayed by the stoic Norn was good or bad, Brynhildr rushed to explain. "Since Strix was so close to you, I thought it might be a good idea to have part of him close with you all the time.

You liked flying with him so much, and, well, I don't like the idea of you using Freyja's falcon suit. I just thought Strix would have wanted you to use his feathers instead of some other bird. It isn't supposed to be a—"

Skuld held up her hand to signal the Valkyrie to stop talking. The girl's voice faded as she watched the Norn gingerly lifted a finely crafted cloak of owl skin out of the wrapping of homespun linen. She held it up to the light, noticing and cherishing the familiar patterns laid out on the feathers. The cloak clasped with a silver round pin engraved with an image of an owl in mid-flight on the top.

When the silence stretched out too long, Brynhildr whispered, "Do you like it?"

There were no words. Skuld loved it and hated it all at once. She loved it because of the sentimental and practical reminder of Strix and his sacrifice for her. And she hated it for being a concrete reminder of her loss. Mostly the thoughtfulness and caring the Valkyrie displayed rendered her speechless.

Fighting back the tears springing to her eyes, Skuld got up from the table with the cloak clutched in her hands and ran out of the hall. Brynhildr remained where she sat, wondering why she'd made such a foolish mistake.

Skuld dodged through the crowds of slain warriors, the Valkyries, the Jǫtnar who came to join the cause, and the dwarves dropping off the final orders of weapons until she came to a secluded hill just out of sight of Valhǫll.

It was quiet out there in the bright, moon-lit night. For as many people crowded Óðinn's great hall, their noise and their lights could not reach so far. Skuld settled herself at the top of the hill and gazed upwards. She missed her home. She missed her sisters. She missed Strix. What started out to be such a simple mission had turned into an incredible mess.

As she gazed up into the night sky at the distant stars and galaxies, she remembered how close they seemed hanging from the branches of the World Tree. As she tried to visualize the plumes of colored dust and gas of the neighboring galaxies, a small tug pulled at her heart. Faint at first, it steadily grew stronger until Skuld could no longer ignore it.

It was a familiar feeling. A feeling of home. The realization of what called to her heart brought Skuld to her feet. The water from the wells. Not just the Well of Destiny, but also from Niðhǫggr's well and the Well of Wisdom.

It must be the waters that were stolen from them, she thought. They had been mixed together and their combined powers sang to her very bones. With how faint the pull was, they were almost far enough for her to not feel them, but still within range. That meant Freyja must also be near. Was this what she and Evyndr stole the well waters for? To turn the tide in the war between the Æsir and the Vanir?

Closing her eyes, she listened to the tug at her heart, focusing on the sensation of the water. It came from the east, near the edge of Ásgarðr and Vanaheimr where the battle would take place come the dawn.

With a bittersweet sigh, Skuld donned the short cloak made of Strix's skin. When it clasped around her neck, instead of transforming her into a mirror image of her beloved owl, the cloak morphed into wings that sprouted out of her back. The transformation was relatively painless, though it took a minute to get used to balancing with large wings attached to her back. Once she mastered that, there were a few failed attempts at flight to gain an understanding of how to work the wings. Soon though she became airborne, soaring towards the battlefield.

She landed in one of the trees near the field, not wanting to be too conspicuous to the thief. Folding her wings behind her, she grabbed her dagger, ready to attack should the need arise.

A small fire illuminated a lone figure on the other side of the glen. The soft sound of drumming and an indistinct chant could be heard in the wind.

Skuld descended from her perch to creep closer towards the fire. She kept her head low and her weapon at the ready. The closer she got, the clearer the voice became. The tenor and pitch were too low for the goddess of beauty. No, instead Evyndr performed this mysterious, rune-less magic. The incantation wove together into a spell by music and the beat of the drums. While the actions were foreign, the words were distinct and plain enough to understand.

"Fall unworthy Æsir, rise noble Vanir. Change the fate carved by runes no one can read. Follow the song of what will be. Fall unworthy Æsir, your time is done. Rise noble Vanir, your time has begun."

As he sang and drummed out the dread tattoo of change, he paused to mix components into a drinking horn. The last thing added was liquid from an otter's skin.

Giving the horn a swirl to combine its contents, Evyndr raised the drinking horn and addressed the sky, repeating his chant one last time and adding one more line. "Fall unworthy Æsir, rise noble Vanir. Change the fate carved by runes no one can read. Follow the song of what will be. Fall unworthy Æsir, your time is done. Rise noble Vanir, your time has begun. I will be the cause of the Æsir's fall, I will raise up the Vanir. Fate is mine to command and I command it to follow me."

Skuld heard enough. Her rage would not allow her to keep quiet and still any longer. It was time to put a stop to this insolence. She etched a rune of amplification in front of her lips. When the power flared, she let out an unearthly shriek which could have woken the dead. The sound echoed around the clearing, successfully obscuring its source. Skuld ran forward, her dagger at the ready.

The abrupt scream echoes disrupted the melodic chant, breaking the power that built up and sending it skittering out into the realms. The unexpected noise made Evyndr jump which spilled the contents of the drinking horn onto the grass.

In an attempt to pinpoint the origin of the noise, he whirled around in a confused circle until he saw Skuld running straight for him. Evyndr clasped a pendant that hung from his neck by a strip of leather. He sang a chant under his breath and the air in front of him shimmered. Right before Skuld's eyes, he disappeared.

Skuld blinked in disbelief. Just like that he vanished. Fury made her scream once more. With the anger heating the blood in her veins, she closed her eyes and tried to feel for the well waters. If they led her here, then they could lead her to wherever Evyndr escaped.

However, the well water no longer called to her. It had also vanished.

Out of sheer frustration, she ransacked the makeshift ceremony spot, throwing the containers of herbs and stones and other magical bric-a-brac. The fire was extinguished with a few kicks of dirt.

When she spent her energy and she destroyed all that was left of Evyndr's presence, she allowed herself to collapse onto the earth and stare at the sky.

Once again, he slipped through her fingers.

But now she understood some of his game. For whatever the reason, he tried to change the predetermined fate that she had carved into the trunk of Yggdrasil so many times before. This was a personal attack.

Still, it didn't take fate to know where Evyndr would be at dawn. This battle was no longer about the gods. No, it became a struggle between her and Evyndr, and the winner would hold the fate of Yggdrasil in their hands.

~~*~*~*

The sun had yet to make an appearance when the full strength of the Æsir force arrived at the battlefield.

Skuld and Brynhildr stood together between the warriors gathered to fight.

"And you're sure Evyndr will be here?" Brynhildr asked, her face grim as she stared ahead.

"I am sure. He is trying to change fate. We cannot let him. I need to take him back to my home. My sisters and I have to make him reverse the damage he's done or all of the worlds in the great tree will perish."

Brynhildr's expression remained the same, but she unsheathed her sword. "If you promise he will suffer, I will make sure you have him before the ravens have a chance at his eyes."

"I promise," Skuld assured her.

The dawn's first rays of light began to diminish the darkness. Out of the shadows of night, the Vanir army appeared hovering at the opposite edge of the field. Their numbers were shrouded in the heavy mist that blanketed the field which, along with the distant drums echoing the heartbeat of the gathered warriors, created an otherworldly feel over the battleground.

Eager shouts sprang up from the assembled Vanir warriors amplified by the steady staccato of their drums. The tension was palpable accompanied by a strange undercurrent to the anticipation.

The warriors to the left of Skuld shifted their weight from foot to foot. Murmuring broke out amongst them. Doubt seeded itself in their minds. The Vanir were powerful and they had battle magic. Could the Æsir's might ever compare?

"Brynhildr," Óðinn called from his position at the head of the forces.

She pushed her way through the warriors to stand at his side. "Yes, All-Father?"

He beheld the beginning of the great battle before him and leaned down to murmur at the Valkyrie. "Can you feel the enemy is weaving magic over the battle? It's an enchantment I've never seen before. He's manipulating the emotions of the fighters."

"Yes, Skuld and I are targeting him."

The All-Father nodded. "Very good. Then you shall harvest him for me. I would know the magic he commands. It may prove useful in the battles to come."

Brynhildr glanced back at Skuld who scanned the converging armies, oblivious to Óðinn's command.

"Do you understand, Brynhildr?" He pitched his tone low. "Bring me the magic-user alive and you shall be exalted, a leader, first of all the Valkyries."

The offer of glory would redeem her for her cowardice the day before and more. It would raise her high amongst the Valkyries and bring much honor to her name. And yet —

Still watching Skuld, she asked, "If I do not do as you ask? If I fail to harvest the sorcerer?"

A heavy hand settled on the young woman's shoulder. Its weight gave the promise of punishment. "Then you will be imprisoned in flames for the rest of time caught between sleep and death. Do not fail me," Óðinn replied.

At once the weight of his hand left and when she glanced over, she wasn't surprised to see Óðinn had gone to initiate the beginning of the battle.

Ravens circled overhead, eager for the feast about to be laid before them. Óðinn gave no epic speech, nor any words of encouragement to the Æsir warriors. All knew why they were here. All knew glory awaited them. A horn sounded, its deep tones reverberating against Skuld's chest. The shouts from her fellow warriors followed. All were ready to kill. All were ready to die.

Skuld cast a sidelong glance at Brynhildr who made her way back to Skuld's side. Her face had been painted and her golden hair braided intricately. She shouted along with the others, blood lust shining in her eyes. Whatever lingering effects Evyndr's cursed charm remained were well hidden.

A blinding flash overhead drew everyone's attention to a solitary spear soaring above the field.

Skuld had to run or risk being trampled by the men behind her who shoved her forward. Brynhildr ran too, shouting a ferocious battle cry at the top of her lungs.

At first, she heard nothing except those ecstatic screams drowning out the sounds of the birds overhead. Then came the solid crash of armor meeting armor and swords biting into shields. The battle cries gave way to grunts, clangs, and thuds. The mist covering the field evaporated with the heat of the bodies and blood being spilt.

Skuld allowed the warriors around her to engage in the enemies as she nimbly dodged around each attack. She fought for one reason alone.

At last, Skuld found Evyndr. He hid behind the main fighting force, hanging back out of striking distance as he sang and drummed up his peculiar brand of battle magic.

Evyndr evoked fear and paranoia. He sang into existence debilitating sorrow and regret, shame and resentment. With every beat of his drum and with every note he sang, the emotions he generated spiraled out into the battlefield. All of Óðinn's warriors within hearing distance of Evyndr faltered in their steps. They flinched away from Vanir blows and even retreated out of the clash. The Æsir lost their fierceness as they allowed their emotions to override their battle cunning.

The spell broke through the battle crazed blood lust which defined the Æsir fighters, leaving them terrified husks of what they once were. Warriors dropped their weapons and begged for death at the hands of their enemies for the shame was too much to bear.

"Brynhildr!" Skuld shouted above the melee of

clashing weapons.

The Valkyrie looked to the Norn, gore and blood spattering her face and hair.

Skuld pointed to where Evyndr stood, drumming and singing. "He's there."

Brynhildr craned her neck to see where Skuld pointed. At the sight of the Vanir, the Valkyrie's lips curled in anger and disgust. She began to charge forward, intent on getting to him and getting in a few good swings before Skuld could take him away. But Skuld held out her arm, gesturing for her to wait.

"He'll see us coming. We need to distract him," Skuld told her.

"How will we do that?"

"You to attack him outright," Skuld said. "I'll sneak up on him from behind."

The Valkyrie considered their position against their target. Encircling Evyndr were three guards, their weapons and shields drawn and ready to protect their charge. All abstained from battle but remained vigilant. An Æsir fighter fell backward into one of the guards. The Vanir wasted no time in gutting the disoriented Æsir and shoved the body away, unconcerned with where it fell.

"It'll be difficult. Those guards around him look fierce. I don't know if I can take all of them at once." She spat on the ground, irritated beyond measure. "Bodyguards in a battle. What a coward."

Skuld glanced around at the fight raging all around them. "We need a distraction for the distraction," she muttered to herself. A loud boom of thunder gave her the solution she'd been searching for. "Where's Þórr?"

The Valkyrie gestured off towards the left. "There. He's swarmed by elves."

Looking over, Skuld calculated the distance, trying to judge if what she had in mind would be feasible. As it turned out, he was closer to Evyndr by about half the distance the two women were.

"We have to get to Þórr," she said, making the decision. "He can take care of those guards for us."

Together, the two made their way through the chaos of clashing weapons and grappling opponents. There was no rhyme or reason for the carnage. Gore slicked the ground making it difficult to keep balance. Skuld had to step carefully while dodging other fighters. She and Brynhildr slashed and cut their way over to where Þórr battled four elven warriors brandishing long, slender swords.

The Valkyrie threw herself into the fray while Skuld employed her runes to repel other fighters from the area.

The elves that were clustered around the God of Thunder fought back against the newcomers with equal ferocity. Þórr, for his part, laughed as though this were just another chance meeting in the woods.

"I am glad to see you two survived Jǫtunheimr." He swung the hammer he wielded in a wide arc, slamming one of the elves viciously in the gut.

Brynhildr grunted as she dodged a stab. She retaliated by cutting deep into her attacker's outstretched arm with her blade.

Skuld smiled at the god in acknowledgement. "See that man over there? The one with the drum, surrounded by bodyguards?" She nodded to where Evyndr stood.

Þórr craned his neck to see over the head of an opponent rushing at him with his sword ready to strike. With a grunt, Þórr swung his hammer into the blade. There was enough force behind it to send the attacker veering off course. Þórr kicked him for good measure before answering, "Yes, I see him. Do you want me to kill him?"

"No, he's the spell caster who is damaging our warriors. He is mine, but Brynhildr and I need you to take out the guards."

Þórr glanced over at his target one more time. "You mean all three at once?"

"Just long enough for Brynhildr to get close enough to distract him from his spell."

The confused furrow appearing on the god's brow made it evident her plan wasn't getting through. "Are you sure you don't want me to kill him? He looks small enough. It wouldn't take me long."

An elf jumped onto the god's back in a vain attempt to tackle him to the ground. A look of annoyance crossed Þórr's face as he wrenched the bold fighter over his shoulder and onto the ground with a thud. A swift smash with his hammer ensured that the elf would not move again.

Skuld replied, her patience wearing thin, "I told you, he's mine. When Brynhildr attacks him, I am going to come at him from the opposite direction. You just focus on the guards and give Brynhildr a chance to get past them."

Þórr gave a good-natured shrug. "Alright, easy enough. Get ready."

Before Skuld could ask for what, Þórr grabbed hold of the nearest attacking elf. Conking him on the head with his hammer, the god proceeded to swing him around in a circle twice before flinging him into the air just above the fighter's heads. With uncanny accuracy, the hapless elf flew the thirty feet to the target and collided straight into two of the three guards surrounding Evyndr.

"I'll send more over soon, but you best hurry." Þórr grinned at Skuld before continuing his own fight.

As she turned to alert Brynhildr, the Norn found the Valkyrie already sprinting towards their target. Skuld hastily put on the owl skin cloak and took to the sky. She circled the battlefield, keeping a keen eye on her friend and the progress she made. When the time was right, she would swoop down behind Evyndr.

Brynhildr waited for Þórr to send another hapless enemy careening into the guards — this time impacting all three as the one who had been spared previously tried to help the others up. This second aerial assault knocked a couple of the guards out, leaving one still conscious at the bottom of a pile of inert bodies. The Valkyrie took her opportunity to attack the Vanir spell caster.

Evyndr barely had enough time to bring his drum up as a shield. It broke under Brynhildr's blade, the taut hide and wooden ring shattering. She kept up her attack, forcing Evyndr farther and farther away from his stumbling guards. As he staggered backward, the concentration he'd been pouring into his spell work disappeared.

At once the effects of his battle magic dissipated. Æsir warriors roared back into the fight. Instead of cowering and begging to die, they attacked with all the viciousness they could muster. Vanir warriors quaked, no longer as confident as they had been at the outset of the battle.

Seeing the tide of the battle turn, Evyndr withdrew a short sword from its sheathe around his waist and used it to defend himself against Brynhildr's unrelenting attacks.

Skuld came up behind the Vanir spell caster, landing a dozen feet away.

Evyndr swung his sword with no real calculation of hitting a target. To his credit, when Brynhildr cut him on the chest, he did not cry out. Instead, he redoubled his clumsy efforts. He got over his initial shock of being attacked and began calculating his moves. No longer purely reactionary, he moved with more care. He created a rhythm with his movements and soon began to chant. Soft at first, it grew steadily louder.

Though the rhythm was different from before, Skuld understood what he intended. She had to act before the targeted enchantment brought her friend down.

Skuld sprinted towards Evyndr.

When Brynhildr did not falter, Evyndr realized the spell he wove wasn't going to work. He had to escape.

Evyndr's hand lifted to grasp the amulet that hung

around his neck.

Brynhildr saw Skuld leap for Evyndr from behind. A brief twitch of her lips betrayed her smile. She twisted so her sword came down just to the left of her target. Skuld wrapped her arms around the unknowing enchanter and shoved him forward onto his face at Brynhildr's feet. They landed hard, but Skuld had been prepared for that.

"Help me hold him," she said to her friend.

Evyndr chose that moment to pitch his weight backward to throw Skuld off of him. He jumped to his feet, ready to bolt.

Brynhildr kicked the man in the face, feeling the crunch of his nose breaking through the leather of her boot. Two more kicks sent him tumbling back onto his stomach, blacked out.

Brynhildr looked down at the unconscious man, a mixture of disgust and conflict affixed to her face. She had to decide what to do and quickly. Should she obey Óðinn and bring him the sorcerer or should she allow Skuld to take him and save Yggdrasil?

"Brynhildr?" Skuld asked, noting the look of indecision in her friend's eyes.

The Valkyrie shook herself at the sound of her name. Looking over at Skuld, she heaved a sigh. "I am going to be in so much trouble for this."

"What?"

Evyndr stirred. Painfully, he brought his hand up to his chest, towards the amulet. For the first time, Skuld understood what he would do.

"Stop him!" she shouted.

Both she and Brynhildr lunged towards Evyndr. As they grabbed hold of him, a bright light flared and all three vanished from the battlefield.

Chapter Ten: Breaking Destiny

In the blink of an eye, the battlefield transformed into lush green vegetation. Vibrant flowers of a million colors climbed up leafy vines. The trees did not grow straight up, but instead took a more meandering path to small patches of sunlight that filtered down through the canopy of taller trees. Thick moss grew on their trunks and dripped off of them like green waterfalls. In place of rocks, there were exposed roots of the trees and the smell of rotting leaves. The sky hid from sight behind dense foliage.

Evyndr, Brynhildr, and Skuld appeared on a carpet of grass instead of soggy, blood-soaked earth.

The heat made Skuld wish her boots were not lined in fur and that she had something lighter to wear. Her lungs labored to breathe in air so humid; it felt as though she were breathing water.

Equally stunned by the unexpected change in scenery, Brynhildr let go of her grip on Evyndr's arm and stared in awe at her surroundings.

"Skuld?" she asked, her voice small. "Where are we?"

"I don't know." Neither she nor her sisters ever guessed at the existence of this realm.

Evyndr rolled to his side, gasping in pain.

The sound brought Skuld back to her senses. Quick as she could, she flipped him onto his back and pinned him to the ground with her knee on his chest. After ripping the amulet from his neck, she hissed with fury behind each syllable, "Where are we?"

Evyndr coughed and spat out the blood that filled his mouth.

Skuld decided she couldn't afford any mistakes. Still holding Evyndr in place, she told Brynhildr, "We need to restrain him."

Glancing around for something that would work as a rope, Brynhildr grabbed a nearby hanging vine. With a mighty tug, it came loose.

Desperate not to be bound, Evyndr heaved Skuld's knee away from his chest. When her weight no longer restrained him, he rolled out of both Brynhildr and Skuld's reach.

Skuld landed hard on her back against the strange, squishy ground.

The Vanir jumped to his feet, his breath heavy and hard. Now that he had the upper hand, the sorcerer began singing a soft chant in a language Skuld didn't quite recognize. As the notes floated into the air, Brynhildr dropped the vine and stared straight ahead. Her mouth went slack and she swayed gently back and forth.

Alarm bells rang violently in Skuld's head, breaking against the sudden feelings of lassitude which engulfed her. She gripped the handle of her dagger and, using all of her strength, she carved the only bind-rune she could think of to counteract Evyndr's magic.

The haunting melody cut off as abruptly as it began. The chirping of bugs obscured the terrified muffled shouts. In place of Evyndr's mouth was a patchy swath of skin. The spell had proven to be effective on Loki, Skuld figured it would be the safest way to gag Evyndr as well.

Clearing her head with a brisk shake, Brynhildr came back to herself. "What happened?"

"Evyndr tried to enchant us," Skuld said as she wrenched the Vanir's hands behind her back. "I figured if he couldn't sing, he couldn't control us with his magic."

Snarling, Brynhildr stalked towards their captive, her sword drawn. With a barely controlled swing, the Valkyrie brought down the blade onto his left ankle. The powerful stroke bit into the flesh and bone with a sickening crunch. Blood sprayed out from the wound as Brynhildr pried the sword out of the flesh and swung again and again until his foot had been completely severed.

Without a mouth, Evyndr couldn't scream. Frantic, pain-filled moans emanated from his chest as he toppled back to the ground.

"What did you do that for?" Skuld hissed and moved to staunch the bleeding. The last thing she needed was for Evyndr to die before getting him back to her sisters.

Brynhildr watched Evyndr shake and tremble as he went into shock, her lips curled in disgust. "Now he can't run either."

Picking up the vine she dropped, Brynhildr used it to bind Evyndr's hands behind his back, holding on to the end of it.

Skuld healed the skin at the site of amputation to stop the bleeding. She didn't reattach the foot because Brynhildr had a point; he couldn't run with only one foot.

"How do we get back?" Brynhildr asked.

Skuld stood and held up the amulet she wrested away from their captive's neck. "I don't know, but this is how we got here. Evyndr murmured some sort of incantation and touched this right before we transported here. Wherever here is."

Both of the women examined the heavy object. It had a triangular design with odd lines and small circles etched into the bronze.

Brynhildr made a distrustful face at the talisman. "Can it take us back?"

"I'll try." Palming the bronze in her hands, Skuld closed her eyes and pictured the Well of Destiny as clearly as she could in her mind. The tug of its power in her chest pointed her more and more behind her and to the left.

Opening her eyes, she glanced in that direction. Barely discernable from the oddly shaped trees and thick, hanging moss was the gentle flapping of a brightly colored fabric against the deep greens of the jungle. Peering as best she could around the greenery, more of the fabric came into view. It seemed to be some sort of strange tent or dwelling. It wasn't animal hide, but it seemed to be fabric very similar to the kind she'd found in Ratatǫskr's teeth.

"This way," she said, motioning for Brynhildr to follow.

"What about him?" she asked, motioning to where Evyndr sat stunned on the ground.

"Let's tie him to a tree so he won't get away. I need to see what's over there."

The man was in too much shock to fight back as the two women bound him both hand and foot to an overgrown tangle of thick branches.

Together Brynhildr and Skuld made their way to the clearing. Even though their destination had been a few yards away, the heat depleted their energy far faster than anticipated.

The fabric tent Skuld had spied through the dense tree line had been just a small portion of the structure dominating the clearing. Curtains of fine woven silk fluttered in the hot, damp breeze. Somewhere a wind chime tinkled, echoing the birds happily tweeting from the trees.

Skuld unwrapped the shred of fabric from the hilt of Týrfingr and held it up to compare to the silk curtains. Different colors, but the same type of weave.

Beyond the free-flowing curtains hid a ramshackle building made with a combination of uneven pieces of wood and stacks of stones. The flat roof consisted of part canvas and part wide leaves. There didn't seem to be one style of architecture here, but rather a hodge-podge of several different types mashed together to create a shelter Skuld didn't believe to be habitable.

They approached the remains of a campfire ringed in large river stones in front of the building. Clay pots sat delicately to one side of the cold heap of charcoal and ash. The table adjacent to the pots sat covered in what Skuld could only define as junk. Something in the midst of stones, mushrooms, bones, and various bits of tooled leather tugged at her chest.

Amongst the bric-a-brac were three slender glass vials sitting side by side. The power that came off of them resonated within Skuld. Familiarity washed over her. Abandoning her caution, she rushed to the table and seized all three of the delicate glass bottles. These were what tugged at her heart. These were what called her in this direction. When they were in her hands, one began to glow as though the contents of it recognized her presence.

"Well waters," Skuld murmured.

Disappointed she hadn't found a way out, she put them into her bag for safekeeping.

"Skuld," Brynhildr called, an odd, uneasy tremor in her voice.

"What is it?" She turned to see what her friend wanted.

Freyja held a disarmed Brynhildr and held her tightly against her, a sharp dagger pressed against the Valkyries neck.

Except it wasn't the same Freyja they met in Vanaheimr. This Freyja was older; the scars of her horrific treatment at the hands of the Æsir long since healed. Bound in a braid, her thick red-gold hair spilled over her shoulder and her eyes were rimmed in black kohl. She did not wear the garb of a warrior though. Her ankle-length dress showed her bare feet and from her belt dangled many pouches.

At her side crouched the biggest feline Skuld had ever seen; its deep golden color and large black spots patterned into its fur blended well with the sun-dappled surroundings.

"If you want your Valkyrie friend to live, then heal my son, Norn."

Skuld's mind raced to understand. "Your son?" she asked, squinting her eyes at the Vanir goddess. "How is this possible? You are not the Freyja of this cycle."

Freyja pressed the blade deeper into Brynhildr's skin, drawing blood. "Do you really want to waste more time asking questions?"

Getting the hint, Skuld backed towards the edge of the clearing where the once captive Vanir sat. His bonds had been cut and he leaned against another giant cat, this one black as midnight. The animal made Skuld hesitate. She noted the massive head — easily bigger than hers — and imagined the teeth waiting just inside its mouth.

"Nava will not harm you," Freyja assured her. "So long as you heal him and cause no further injury."

Evyndr glared at the Norn as she knelt at his side. The swath of skin loosened and gaped enough to form the suggestion of lips, though there still wasn't an opening. Her spell had almost worn off.

Skuld paused, turning to regard the goddess. "Before I return his powers of speech, I need to know why you are changing fate. Why are you killing Yggdrasil?"

The Vanir goddess shook her head. "Heal him and I will tell you."

Not seeing any other choice without sacrificing Brynhildr, Skuld uncarved the bind-rune, removing the swath of skin with Evyndr's mouth.

"Mother!" he cried out.

"Quiet," she told him. Keeping her eyes on Skuld, she ordered, "Now his foot."

"You promised an explanation," Skuld countered.

"Why do you defy destiny?"

Evyndr's eyes narrowed. "She did not defy destiny. I am the breaker of destinies!" he spat. The flush of his own anger and self-vindication ran through him. The words poured out of him in a heated stream of words, each delivered with a jabbing force as though he could harm her with the sharpened syllables. "I alone have the magic that can break your hold over the Nine Realms."

"Evyndr, enough!" Freyja shouted.

"What magic? What have you done, you cur?" Skuld wrapped her fingers in his hair to pull his face back so he looked directly into his face. A wild gleam twinkled in his eyes that Skuld didn't like. They shone brighter than they should and she thought she saw a glimpse of obsession and great pain in their depths.

"Take your hands off my son or this Valkyrie will pay the price, Norn," Freyja swore. The desperation in her voice made it apparent the situation slipped out of her control.

Brynhildr remained as quiet and as calm as she could, waiting for an opportunity to flip the odds into their favor.

Skuld paid Freyja no heed. Instead, she focused on Evyndr. "What fate do you think you have? I am the one who carves destiny into the great tree. I am the keeper of what should be in every life. Your future holds pain and blood to undo this disaster you have wrought."

"It is already done! The Æsir will lose the war and the Vanir will take their rightful place as the supreme tribe of gods. The fate you and your sisters carve will be broken. We are no longer slaves to your whims."

Rage made Skuld's grip on the insolent man tremble. "How? How could you do such a foolish, disastrous thing?"

Sensing the Norn was at the end of her patience, Freyja ordered, "Step away from him now!" She jerked Brynhildr backward.

"Do you realize what you two have done?" Skuld shouted. "Do you understand Yggdrasil is dying because of your desire to create your own future?"

Freyja joined the argument, her passion emerging. "Do you understand what torture you put the peoples of the realms through, Norn? I suffered greatly at the hands of the Æsir. I was tortured, raped, and brought to the brink of death. If that were not enough, I was traded as a hostage after losing the war. So many of my people were killed in an attempt to gain reparation for the way I had been treated. My suffering was so great, my tears turned to gold.

"When I learned I was pregnant after my assault, I decided I could not allow the Nornir to make my child suffer as much as I had. I found this place and we stayed outside of the cycles, outside of time." Freyja let her hand with the knife drop slightly as she expressed her anger at the misery she'd endured.

The Valkyrie took advantage of the momentary imbalance of her captor. With incredible speed, she slammed her boot down onto Freyja's bare feet. As she did, she twisted the arm with the knife and danced out of the goddess's grasp.

From the ground, she picked up her sword and, with a scant breath in between, she charged at Freyja.

The goddess recovered from the unexpected pain and had just enough time to sing a barrier into existence between her and the charging Valkyrie. Brynhildr's sword glanced off of the obstruction.

Freyja sang another enchantment. The ground trembled, rumbled, and cracked, opening up right beneath Brynhildr. The Valkyrie slipped, but grabbed hold of Freyja's dress, rippling it on her way down.

"Brynhildr!" Skuld screamed. She rushed to the aid of the Valkyrie.

When she reached the edge of the pit, she saw her friend crumpled at the bottom, unconscious from the fall.

As Skuld searched for a way to get Brynhilde out, the joined voices of Freyja and her son rose in full melodic harmony. The song wove in and out of her thoughts. It plucked the chords of her emotions, playing them in rapid succession. Fear, despair, shame, doubt, guilt, and helplessness cycled through her. Wave after wave of unrelenting mood changes paralyzed her with inaction.

Something smooth brushed against her legs. It slowly wound its way around her limbs, pulling them together tighter and tighter.

Skuld managed to glance down and found a multitude of thick vines encircled her, trapping her in place. The smooth vines soon became rough and prickled. Those prickles became thorns which embedded themselves deep into Skuld's skin.

The Norn struggled, only to be bitten by more thorns. The stings amplified her fear until her heart thudded in her chest and panic set in.

The vines didn't stop once she became immobilized; they slithered her into the pit, suspending her just above the bottom.

Freyja and Evyndr's song came to an end.

"What shall we do with them?" Evyndr asked, hate lacing his words. "Kill them?"

"The Valkyrie, yes. However, we cannot kill a Norn," Freyja replied. "We haven't the strength required."

"But the well water! I can drink them all together. That would amplify my powers enough to kill her."

Freyja scoffed. "And how then would we go about changing the fate of the realms if you wasted the well waters on killing a Norn? No. We need to stick to the plan."

She fell into a thoughtful silence. "However, we can make the Norn watch destiny unravel. She'll be helpless and will suffer just as we have suffered watching her control cycle after cycle of destruction."

Skuld could almost see Evyndr grin at the idea. A few

feet away from her, Brynhildr groaned and stirred.

"That is a brilliant idea, Mother."

"Yes, it almost makes up for you bungling the retrieval of the well water in the first place. We have one chance to get this right. Lets' get what's left of the well water and then we will send you back into the battle. We cannot afford to make any more mistakes." Both Freyja and Evyndr moved away from the top of the pit.

As the comprehension of what she'd heard filtered through the chaotic emotions inside of her, the puzzle pieces of why water from all three of Yggdrasil's wells and how they could be used clicked into place. If Evyndr could use the waters to amplify his powers, then Skuld could do the same. She could restore her magic and get them out of this mess.

"Brynhildr!" she hissed. "Wake up! I need you!"

The Valkyrie groaned and blinked her eyes open.

"Hurry. In my bag, there are three vials of water. I need you to pour them into my mouth."

"What?" Bleary-eyed and confused, Brynhildr stared at her friend. "Why are you covered in vines?"

"Never mind! Just get me the vials and quick! They will be back soon when they can't find them."

The Valkyrie lurched to her feet and stumbled the few steps to where Skuld hung suspended. It took longer than Skuld preferred and Brynhildr exclaimed every time she pricked her skin on one of the thorns, but, in time, the three vials were rescued from the depths of the leather bag.

A crash sounded from somewhere in the clearing above. "Where are they, Evyndr? Where did you put the well waters?"

They were running out of time. Skuld told Brynhildr. "Alright, pour the water into my mouth.

"Which one?"

"All of them! Now!" She opened her mouth wide and waited impatiently.

Brynhildr unstoppered the vials and poured them all into Skuld's mouth at once.

She choked a little at first, but managed to gulp all of the sweet, fresh liquid down. The power of the well waters revived her dwindling energy as soon as the first drop slid down her throat. The more she drank, the more she was restored.

The effects of each of the wells flooded through her. Mímisbrunnr, the Well of Wisdom gave her insight and understanding into Freyja and Evyndr's actions. Hvergelmir, the Well of Creation and Memory, showed her the shoot of a branch on Yggdrasil missed by the grazing deer. A pregnant Freyja stumbling upon the realm by chance and hiding there for cycles. It showed her the root of the path they were on. The Well of Destiny returned her rune magic and her powers of foresight.

A gasp from Brynhildr made Skuld shift her gaze to her friend.

"Skuld, what's happening to you? There are runes all over your skin! They're glowing!"

Instead of answering, Skuld said, "Cut me down. Freyja and Evyndr will return soon. We need to be ready."

Her friend did as she asked. When the vines were severed, the thorns extracted themselves out of her skin and fell to the ground. The runes glowed even more fiercely.

"It's time to get out of here. Do you have your swan skin?"

Awestruck at the evident changes in Skuld, Brynhildr nodded.

"Good. Go for Evyndr. Don't kill him, but make sure he can't sing. I will handle Freyja."

Brynhildr nodded once and pulled on her feathered cloak. Her transformation was different though; instead of turning fully into a swan, the Valkyrie sprouted wings out of her back.

At Skuld's asking glance, Brynhildr shrugged, "This is the new style with the Valkyries. It's easier to fight with arms. I traded in my old skin for a new one when I had them make yours." Without another word, she took flight.

Shaking her head, Skuld donned her feathered cloak and followed.

Both Freyja and Evyndr were at the crowded table, overturning and shifting the items in desperate search of the vials. Both of their backs were to the pit, so neither witnessed the escape.

Both Norn and Valkyrie attacked at once. Brynhildr dove at Evyndr, knocking him to the ground. Skuld flew right behind Freyja, her dagger raised to draw a bind-rune. She confined both of them inside a magic barrier. While it limited her movements, the trap would debilitate Freyja's fertility magic more.

Freyja lifted her voice in song, summoning whatever plant life she could into the confined space. While none could breach Skuld's barrier, vines, grass, flowers, and moss grew so thick they covered the shield spell, creating a dome of vegetation.

"Your life should have ended long ago," Skuld said.

Freyja stood tall and proud. "My life is my own. My destiny is my own. I will not submit to your rules." The goddess lunged forward, her dagger jabbing towards Skuld's stomach.

The runes on Skuld's skin flared as she shifted to the left. Her reaction was a moment too slow; the dagger scraped her arm, leaving a faint trail of blood in its wake.

Recovering her balance, Freyja narrowed her eyes. "You drank the well waters."

Skuld didn't move, merely waited in silence.

"The powers won't last. Soon they will fade and you will become vulnerable once again. All I have to do is wait you out. I've become very good at waiting."

"Not unless I kill you," Skuld replied.

The goddess gave a mirthless laugh. "You cannot kill

me unless you carve it into Yggdrasil. Do not be surprised I know this. I've used these long cycles to learn all about you and your sisters. You are useless when you walk the realms, that's why you avoid doing it."

Skuld couldn't listen to anymore. With sharp, deft movements and a heart full of rage, she hefted Týrfingr from her belt and rushed for Freyja.

The goddess twirled around, avoiding the point of the blade, and slashed at her opponent as she danced away.

This did nothing to quell the rage building in Skuld's chest. Moving as quickly as she could, she whirled to meet Freyja head-on.

As Skuld turned the point of the sword back towards her, Freyja kicked loose dirt into Skuld's eyes before twisting as far out of range as she could.

Skuld blinked and wiped at the dirt obscuring her vision. Enough of this!

Freyja moved behind Skuld, her dagger at the ready.

The Norn disappeared right before her eyes.

In a flash, Skuld reappeared in front of her, impaling Týrfingr into her chest.

The goddess let out a surprised gurgle. She stared at Skuld, not comprehending what happened.

"Your destiny will always be mine to carve, Freyja."

As her life faded from her eyes, the dome of plants withered and cracked, the debris falling around the protective barrier in heaps.

Skuld pulled Týrfingr from the goddess's chest. She removed the barrier and emerged from the seclusion, ready to end this mission. All that remained was getting Evyndr back to her sisters and putting an end to this senseless destruction.

"Skuld!" Brynhildr cried out in relief. She held Evyndr pinned with the point of her sword against the outside wall of the hut. Both panted from their prolonged fight. A sheen of sweat plastered Brynhildr's hair to her forehead.

"Mother!" Evyndr screamed when he saw Freyja's corpse and the fast-growing pool of blood beneath it.

All of Skuld's patience vanished. A wave of her hand sealed his lips shut so that only muffled sounds replaced his shouts.

"We need to get him to my sisters."

A loud roar followed by a yellow and black blur cut off Brynhildr's response. The giant cat tackled the Valkyrie to the ground. She dropped her sword as she brought up her hands to cover her head against large teeth and claws.

The sight of a cat bigger than her caused Skuld a flutter of panic in her chest. Nevertheless, she rushed forward to help Brynhildr a bind-rune already being traced in the air. The cat yipped as though it had been stung and it turned its dark eyes to the Norn as it leapt at her.

Before its extended claws could reach her, Skuld drew another bind-rune, freezing the creature in a block of ice mid-leap. With a clatter, the ice fell to the dirt, melting in the humid air of the jungle.

She ran around the frozen cat and straight for her friend.

Evyndr reached the shaking Valkyrie first. He stood over her with her sword in his hands. Tears streamed down his cheeks, but without a mouth, he couldn't sing the spell to make her suffer nearly enough.

Skuld saw what he would do. The flash of the sword in the jungle afternoon light seemed surreal. Desperate to stop him, Skuld threw rune after rune into the air. None of them worked.

Glancing at her arms, she saw the runes in her skin fading away. The power of the well waters was gone.

She was too slow to stop Evyndr from sinking Brynhildr's sword into her stomach.

Brynhildr cried out in shock and pain.

Skuld collided with Evyndr, knocking him to the ground. Her fists moved on their own, slamming into his face over and over again. He sagged under her, his limbs falling limp.

She wanted to kill him. She wanted to take his life as he took Brynhildr's.

But if she didn't get him to her sisters, then Yggdrasil itself would die.

The reminder of everything at stake subdued Skuld's rage, but only barely. She left the unconscious and bleeding Evyndr on the ground and went to her friend.

Brynhildr trembled on the ground, her hands fluttered around the blade impaled in her stomach.

Skuld pulled the sword away and pressed her hands into the stomach wound. The well water powers were gone, but maybe she could still help.

"Skuld," Brynhildr gasped. "No time. Get Evyndr. Heal Yggdrasil."

"You aren't supposed to die this way!" The frantic rune drawing on her skin illustrated the fear and helplessness in the Norn's voice. "You can't' die, Brynhildr. I need you!"

The Valkyrie raised a shaking hand to Skuld's tear-streaked face. "Find me. Next cycle. Promise." She coughed and drew in shuddering breaths.

Skuld let out a choked sob as Brynhilde struggled to breathe. "I promise."

Brynhildr's arm fell to her side. Her fingers struggled to open a small pouch on her belt. When she brought her hand back up, she pressed her bone dice into Skuld's hand. "Make sure you win," she rasped, her voice fading.

Her hand fell to the ground. Her breath grew faint and her shuddering ceased. She became unearthly still.

Skuld cried unabashedly as her friend let out her last breath.

The black-spotted cat's icy imprisonment disappeared, leaving a drenched and confused animal searching for its prey. The disorientation that kept it on the ground wouldn't last long.

Skuld pulled herself together. There wasn't time to bury Brynhildr. She had a mission to fulfill.

Unable to stay in the clearing, she donned her feather skin and picked up the unconscious Evyndr. As a precaution, she bound him with long strips of the fabric fluttering from the openings of the dwelling. Even though he remained unconscious and only one foot, she didn't want to risk him getting away any longer. She flew away from the clearing quickly, avoiding the damp feline as best she could.

The added weight of her immobilized captive didn't allow for significant clearance from the ground, much less the ability to rise above the thick canopy of the jungle. As a result, she flew slower than she wanted and had to dodge the tangled foliage.

Before long, Skuld's arms began to ache. Her wings strained to keep her pace, but they weakened with every movement. The suffocating heat drenched her in sweat and, as a result, her grip on Evyndr kept slipping.

They came to rest among a tangle of roots along the jungle floor. It didn't matter how far she got from the clearing; the only way out of this realm was the amulet. She pulled it out of her pocket and turned the bronze talisman over in her hands.

Evyndr stirred.

"Bausi! Nava!" he yelled.

Startled and fearing he cast a spell with his strange magic, Skuld rushed over to him and clamped her hand down on his returned mouth. Her rune faded.

"None of that sorcery. I will get you back to my sisters and we will put right the many wrongs you have committed."

An audible rustling made the Norn freeze in place. Keeping her hand against Evyndr's mouth, Skuld twisted to look over her left shoulder. Staring back at her, the giant black feline crouched, its muscles shifted as it prepared to strike. It watched her with large golden eyes, waiting for her to make a move.

Above them, birds sang out in a panic.

Skuld rolled out of the way just as the cat landed on its feet where she had once been. The creature lashed out with its claws extended and teeth bared. A primal growl accompanied the attack as the sharp claws sliced into her shin.

She let out a hiss of pain even as she scrambled backward over exposed tree roots to get away. Her hands smashed into mushroom caps, making her slip onto her back, cracking her head on a rotting log. Her wings throbbed with pain at being twisted in unnatural ways.

Cursing under her breath, Skuld flipped to her stomach and brought the bronze talisman closer to her face. How did this thing work? The sigils carved into it were foreign and she didn't have the slightest idea what they meant.

A black paw reached out from the ferns next to her. The unexpected swipe sent her scurrying forward on her hands and knees. She made it a few feet before powerful jaws latched onto her leg.

She screamed in agony and shock as teeth impaled themselves into her muscles, right down to the bone. The earth moved under her as she was dragged backward over the debris of the jungle floor.

Adrenaline pumped through her body and her fighting instinct for self-preservation gave her courage and enough desperation to kick the cat with her other foot. Every kick that landed, caused the teeth to slide, making the puncture wound in her leg a bigger gouge with more damage. So desperate to get away, she barely felt the pain.

When the giant cat released her. Skuld tried to draw a protective barrier between her and the predator. The runes did not glow; the spell never activated. Too late, she had forgotten that her powers were useless.

She had to get the talisman to work.

Skuld gripped the amulet and murmured a whispered plea. "Please take me home. Take me and this cur to the Well of Destiny where my sisters wait for me."

Nothing happened.

Before she could register her disappointment, the black cat launched itself at her.

She rolled to the side, narrowly missing claws to her face. Her wings took the brunt of the damage. Claws ripped through the magic of the owl skin. She screamed in pain and fury as the feathers were shorn off.

In a frantic move of desperation, Skuld unclasped the owl cloak and wiggled out from under it.

Think! What did Evyndr do when he vanished from the battlefield?

The memory triggered the realization she needed. *He sang.* His magic stemmed from song. *But what song?*

She stood for too long; the force of the cat's impact shoved her and her captive violently forward. The animal's claws dug into her back, slicing downwards. The claws retracted as the cat readjusted to leap again, this time with teeth at the ready.

Skuld fell forward and tried to catch herself mid-fall. Instead, her limbs entangled with Evyndr's. As they tumbled, she let out a quiet, pain-wracked warble of a melody. "Home. Take us home to the Well of Destiny."

As her intent manifested into song, a pale light emanated from the amulet, shining out from between the Norn's fingers. A strange, nauseous feeling swirled in the pit of her stomach. This wasn't like before. Unsure of what was happening, she held on to Evyndr, determined not to let him go.

The light grew brighter and bigger, engulfing both of them. In the middle of her nausea, a twisting sensation wrenched all of her nerves. She closed her eyes to keep herself from being sick.

Chapter Eleven: Consequence

The very air changed; the sweltering humidity disappeared as did the brightness of the day. Squinting her eyes open, Skuld let out a sigh of relief at the familiar sight of the roots of Yggdrasil.

Mindful of the open wounds from the animal attacks, she untangled herself from Evyndr who glowered at his surroundings.

"Sister, you've returned!" a familiar voice called from behind her.

With a wide smile, Skuld turned to face her sister Verðandi and froze in shock. No longer the matronly woman she had been when Skuld departed, Verðandi appeared as though she'd aged a millennium. Shriveled and bent, she supported her weight on a staff. Her clothes sagged around her emaciated frame just as her skin wrinkled and bunched on her face. Her once thick and full head of hair had thinned and fell out in uneven clumps that left pale patches of her scalp exposed.

"Sister," Skuld gasped. "What happened?"

"Is this the scoundrel that befouled our well and poisoned the great tree?"

Evyndr glared up at the ill Norn, defiance etched into his face. "The tyranny of the Nornir is ending!"

Skuld kicked him savagely in the gut to keep him quiet. "He was difficult to catch."

Verðandi gave a solemn nod. "Come. There isn't time

to waste." She left Skuld to bring her captive.

Skuld retied the fabric around Evyndr's hands and arms to make sure he wouldn't escape. "Your magic will not work here, murderer. If you try, I will remove your tongue with my fingers."

Still unable to move, and gasping for air, Evyndr nodded to indicate his understanding.

Yanking on the makeshift rope, she roughly shoved Evyndr onto one of the thick gray leaves to make dragging him easier. They were a short distance to the well, but Skuld was tired and her wounds throbbed with the exertion.

Instead of the usual lush greenery set against the dark, yet vibrantly colored galaxies surrounding Yggdrasil, an ashen gray atmosphere pervaded the area. Too many dead leaves littered the small patch of terrain the Nornir called home. The sight made Skuld sick.

As she dragged Evyndr behind her, Skuld took in the sight of her decaying home with mounting horror. In the short time she had been away, the entire base of Yggdrasil eroded. The roots transformed from a healthy brown to pale and splotchy gray. What's more, the wood became brittle. It crumbled to dust at the slightest pressure, as Skuld discovered the hard way when she climbed over a large root and it fell away beneath her.

Soon enough, the Well of Destiny and the modest hut she and her sisters lived in came into view. With a heavy heart, Skuld beheld the destruction of her home. The well, formerly an abundant spring of crystal-clear water in white nourishing mud, now a dried-up trickle of dingy gray sludge. Ashy dust powdered under their footsteps. The grass just beyond the well had become stiff brown and lifeless.

Waiting near the well sat a hunched heap of clothes. It perched on a boulder next to an oversized staff.

Verðandi approached the stack of clothes and laid a gentle hand on the side of it. "Sister, Skuld finally returned to us. She has brought the murderer for justice."

The pile of clothes shifted to deliberately face where Skuld hoisted Evyndr to his feet. Through the shadows of a deep hood, the young Norn saw the glimmer of her eldest sister's eyes.

"So you have returned," came the breathy whisper. The soft sound of her sister's voice took Skuld aback. It was no longer strong and confident, rather she sounded weak and unsure. The changes in both of her sisters and her home made the young Norn worry she was already too late to fix all of what Evyndr caused.

"What happened here? Why have you both aged so much?"

Urðr reached out a trembling hand to her youngest sister. "Time has shifted. Did you not notice in your travels? As Yggdrasil ailed, so the bonds of time broke among the realms. You have been gone for many cycles, sister."

Swallowing the sudden onslaught of guilt, Skuld replied, "I have brought the one who has wrought all of this woe. Tell me, have you and Verðandi discovered a way to reverse all of this devastation?"

The frail mound of clothes gave a subtle and solemn nod. "We have found a potential solution."

"Though we are far from certain it will work," Verðandi interjected.

"We are out of time," Urðr rasped. "We have prepared everything already. We must proceed as this is our final chance."

Skuld took in a deep breath trying to use her powers to see the outcome of this course in her mind. No runes appeared, no urge to carve anything, no hint of what would be.

"Tell me what needs to be done."

Both of her sisters gave a nod of assent, but Verðandi gave the directions. "We've prepared a space. Bring the murderer to what's left of the well," she gestured with a frail, wrinkled arm towards where the once pristine and nourishing mud once piled. The dry, cracked, ash-colored dirt had been scraped levelly. Bones formed a perimeter around a six-foot area. Inside the border of bones were layers of runes etched into the dirt.

The sight of the squirrel's remains triggered a welling of grief in her heart. Ratatǫskr had been Evyndr's first victim. If this endeavor worked, she would honor him.

"What are you going to do?" Evyndr asked. For the first time, Skuld heard fear in his voice.

Skuld ignored him and instead read through the inscribed sigils, realizing the complexity and riskiness of what her sisters wanted to attempt.

"Reversals and undoings? Sisters, are we really going to attempt to uncarve all of fate itself? This isn't a reversal of one person's fate. This spell would erase all of the destinies of all the Nine Realms. It would obliterate everything we worked so hard to maintain!"

Verðandi assisted Urðr to a spot inside the ritual area where the eldest Norn could sit until they were ready to proceed.

"Believe me when I say there is no other option. We either undo everything or waste away along with Yggdrasil. Enough of this. We do not have time to squabble amongst ourselves. All of our energy, all of our focus needs to be on the task at hand."

Skuld blew out a heavy sigh. "Of course. You are right, sister." Skuld hoisted Evyndr over her shoulders. He shifted and moved as much as he could making Skuld's progress slow and more painful. She maneuvered him to the low wooden altar in the center of the runes and bones.

The altar's surface was just wide enough for Evyndr to kneel on. Deep grooves were carved around the edges. They funneled down into fashioned spouts on both edges of the board and one in the center. Beneath these spouts rested three pink clay pots. The pots must have been made just after the well had been befouled, and its white mud stained with the blood of Ratatǫskr.

Verðandi disappeared into the modest hut as Skuld positioned Evyndr on the altar so he could look up and behold the decay of the great World Tree above them.

The sight of the ritual space and the state of Yggdrasil caused the reality of the situation to hit him.

"No," he moaned. "No, no. I cannot be here. This is not my destiny! I refuse to let this be my fate!" Panicked tears streamed down the man's face and low sobs of realized helplessness echoed in the silence of the well.

"Why does the murderer shed tears?" Urðr called out. "Do the consequences of his actions offend him so?" The fury in her eldest sister's voice reminded Skuld that, like herself, Urðr and Verðandi deserved to know the motivations of Evyndr's actions.

Verðandi emerged from the hut with three daggers made of bone. In the back of her mind, Skuld wondered what else they used Ratatǫskr's body for.

"Why does he not speak?" Urðr demanded, the iron returning to her wispy voice just enough to snap Evyndr's attention upon her.

"Tell them," Skuld prodded. "Tell them why you have killed the great ash tree, Yggdrasil, and all who dwell within it."

Evyndr shook his head in denial of the evidence before him. "No. No, I haven't. I haven't done any such thing."

Skuld leaned down, staring him straight in the eye. "Do you see this place? Do you see my sisters? Yggdrasil is dying because you befouled the Well of Destiny. You murdered Ratatǫskr. You caused Niðhǫggr's sickness and eventual death from the poison you placed in the well he guarded. You murdered Mímir. You are the one who has killed us all."

Evyndr shut his eyes against the truth of Skuld's

words. "I wanted to change the fate of the Vanir. I didn't want this. I didn't want this." The confession came with more tears. "I am sorry. I am so sorry," he repeated over and over again.

A sudden trembling shook the terrain. A rumble echoed from beneath them. Blackened and brittle leaves rained down from above.

"We must begin," Urðr insisted. "We are running out of time."

Verðandi handed each of her sisters a dagger. Upon closer inspection, Skuld saw they were whittled from antler.

Shocked, Skuld glanced at her sister in askance. "The deer?"

A saddened nod affirmed Skuld's suspicions. "Not long ago they succumbed to the poison spreading through Yggdrasil. We are the only ones left outside of the Nine Realms."

"Focus, both of you," Urðr said. "We must harvest the blood of this fateless one and we will use it to fill the runes inscribed on the ground. All of the runes need the sacrificial blood of the one responsible in order to erase what has come before. It will take all three of us and what little power we have left to command the runes."

"How must we harvest his blood?" Verðandi asked.

Urðr considered the question. "Since he is the one who has killed so many, Ratatǫskr, Niðhǫggr, the deer —"

"Brynhildr," Skuld added, interrupting her sister. She swallowed back the grief that lumped into her throat at the sound of her friend's name.

Her sisters exchanged a confused look before Urðr continued, "It is right we exact compensation for their deaths. Their lives were not his to take. For that crime, we will perform the blood eagle as compensation for all which has been lost. Agreed?"

Verðandi said immediately, "Agreed."

Skuld looked at Evyndr, considering everything she

had been through to track him down. All of the deceit, time wasted and all of the damage he selfishly caused.

At last, she said, "It's not enough for what he has done, but it will have to suffice as we do not have the time for a more befitting punishment. His blood will reverse what he has done and heal Yggdrasil."

Evyndr sobbed even harder when he heard their pronouncement and judgement. "No," he moaned in terror.

The sisters ignored his cries.

Urðr shakily got to her feet and, leaning upon her staff, made a few hobbling steps so she could join her sisters at the altar.

Moving in unison, the three sisters took their places; Urðr on the left, Verðandi on the right, and Skuld facing Evyndr's back. Wordlessly, Urðr traced sigils just above Evyndr's skin.

When Urðr finished, the strips of fabric which bound Evyndr vanished, replaced by invisible bonds stretching his arms out wide to either side. He grunted at the tension straining his muscles.

Verðandi and Urðr joined Skuld at Evyndr's back. The three raised their arms, antler daggers still in hand. Verðandi began the supplication.

"Oh, great Yggdrasil, bear witness to this sacrifice. This foolish man thought to defy destiny. The crimes he has committed in the name of this blasphemy are unspeakable. We three sisters, Guardians of the Well of Destiny, the Carvers of Fate, spill his blood to reverse what he has done. Accept this sacrifice and uncarve the destinies of all who live within you so we may make it right again."

When she completed the supplication, all three of the Nornir brought their daggers down into Evyndr's back. Together they carved into his flesh, cutting down to the bones. Blood poured out in thick streams onto the altar. It ran through the grooves chiseled out for precisely that purpose.

Pained whimpers escaped Evyndr's lips through all of this. Skuld hoped he would scream. She wanted to hear the proof of his agony.

When the back of his ribs were exposed, Verðandi took the hilt of her dagger and bludgeoned them. Soft, wet crunches pervaded the air as his bones broke under her ministrations. Pushing the loose pieces aside, she cleared the way for Skuld to do her part.

Then youngest Norn tentatively pushed her fingers into the open wound. He trembled from the inside, yet he stubbornly remained silent. His silence infuriated Skuld. With harsh, jerking motions, she wrapped her fist around his lungs and yanked them out through the cut in his back.

That did it. That harsh, quick movement broke Evyndr's determined dignity. The sound of his screams filled the air for the briefest of moments before fading into wet gurgles and strangled gasping. Evyndr's body shuddered and convulsed a final time before he slumped down, his weight supported by Urðr's enchanted bonds.

Before the blood stopped pumping, Urðr and Verðandi sliced into the nearest artery. The smell of the acrid crimson gush overtook Skuld as she stood there, shaking with the violence. It had been too short, in her opinion. Though, it did give her a grim satisfaction to know he died just as dishonorably as he lived.

"Come, Sister," Urðr rasped. "We must finish the ritual."

Verðandi handed her one of the pink bowls, thick warm blood sloshing up to the inside rim.

The sisters worked their way around the ritual area, anointing the previously etched runes in the dirt with Evyndr's sacrificial blood. Each of the sigils glowed as soon as the blood touched them.

When the last set had been filled, they put down their bowls and joined hands.

Another deep rumble emanated from the ground beneath them. The well with its trickle of muck began bubbling violently, the mud changing from a gray to a deep crimson. A deafening crack filled the air.

Skuld looked around in terror to see the trunk of the great tree split unevenly down its center. The large rift teemed with violent energy released out into the very air.

Skuld heard Urðr scream something, but she couldn't make it out over the sound of wood being split apart from the inside. A gust of wind whipped over the well, blowing the sisters off balance. Skuld fell to the ground atop two sets of the blood-stained runes the trio worked so hard to cast. She knocked her head against a stone. Darkness overtook her.

~~*~*~*

Skuld made her way over the hollowed branches and rotting leaves, the remaining debris of the dead cosmic tree called Yggdrasil. A few of the fallen limbs still held the runes she and her sisters carved so long ago. The memory of her sisters stirred up the old familiar pain. They died not long after the last desperate ritual to stop what Skuld since determined to be inevitable.

That had been so long ago.

Trapped at the base of the corpse of the World Tree, Skuld scavenged to survive. It took a surprising amount of time for Yggdrasil to finally die. One by one, Skuld had watched each of the worlds in the giant tree's branches disintegrate, the remaining matter crumbling down atop of her.

The fires of Múspellsheimr had long been extinguished. The fog of Niflheimr dissipated and its ice melted. The caves of Niðavellir collapsed. Ásgarðr, Miðgarðr, and Vanaheimr winked out of existence like distant stars who gave up their light.

All faded until all that remained was the lifeless husk

of Yggdrasil and a rapidly weakening Norn.

Skuld made her way to where the Well of Destiny had once been. Only a gaping, decaying hole into nothing remained. She often came to the familiar spot to wonder about what could have been if she and her sisters were successful.

If the worlds survived, she would want to explore the realms more and discover the things about its inhabitants that carving their fates wouldn't reveal. She wanted to fly with Strix again. She wanted to see Brynhildr and play the dice game one more time. She would even square off against Óðinn once more if it meant things could go back to the way they were. The memories of her sisters and her friends made the dark, dying world around her seem less lonely.

Time raced past her now, making those memories seem so distant and unattainable.

As she walked, the shadow of something above her crossed over. She lifted her wrinkled face upwards and witnessed the last leaf from the top-most branches float down. Her breath caught in her throat as she watched it fall. A sorrowful resignation washed through her veins. Time for the end.

She finished the short trek to the well, her mind turning over the impossibilities of survival. But when she reached the hole and the great rift in Yggdrasil's trunk, she spotted something unexpected.

Climbing over what remained of the roots, Skuld scrambled to see if what she thought she glimpsed was indeed real. The old bark crumbled at her touch, but she still found purchase on the sturdier parts.

There, at the very corner of the split trunk stood something Skuld could scarcely believe. Out of the dead Yggdrasil grew a small shoot of green with two circular green leaves. Both balanced on a twig no bigger than a blade of grass.

The sight of the green sprout sent a thrill of hope

through Skuld. She let out a cackle of laughter. Giddiness stretched a smile over her lips.

Things would not be the same as they were before, she could tell that much. The sight of the tender shoot made the future spread out before her in all of its limitless possibilities and countless paths. Hope infused her and she grinned, looking forward to carving fate once again.

<u>Afterword</u>

Being a fiction author is not unlike having schizophrenia. Our characters are the voices in our heads who drive us to vivid hallucinations to form alternate realities.

Skuld has been a voice in my head for a long time, longer than I can reckon. Her story simmered in the background for many years, her voice whispering and guiding me. In hindsight, it was her influence that got me into Norse mythology. I always had a passing interest as it is my heritage. However, with Skuld nudging me into that direction, I dug out my mythology books and dove headfirst. What resulted was a multi-year submersion into everything Norse. I listened to Norse music. I read all the Norse stories and legends that I could get my hands on. Norse symbols were tattooed into my skin. I learned some of the language. I drew the line at lutefisk (although my best friend's mom gave me lefse. Thanks, Dawn!)

My descent into everything Norse was (unknowingly) aided and abetted by one Dr. Jackson Crawford. Currently a professor at the University of Colorado, Boulder, he has an extensive YouTube library where he posts videos on Norse language and myth. These videos proved to be invaluable as he offered intrinsic knowledge and insight into the source texts of Norse myth that I could not find anywhere else.

While a ton of research is usually done to make fiction books as realistic as possible, we authors don't typically cite our sources. Here is where I am breaking with tradition because Dr. Crawford is an incredible resource. If you want to know more about the Old Norse language, all of the myths and the source material available for them, look up Dr. Crawford.

I can say definitively, Dr. Crawford's shared knowledge shaped the world in which Skuld needed to exist. Now, hopefully she can get out of my head and live in the pages I wrote.

That being said, please know that any mistakes are mine and mine alone. I have done my utmost to preserve the integrity of the Norse myths and their source material while also allowing Skuld to tell her story. It's a tricky thing to balance.

To summarize: hearing voices might mean you are a writer, lefse is delicious, Norse stuff is awesome, and thank you Dr. Crawford!

Kira has been telling stories for as long as she could talk and writing them down as soon as she could hold a crayon. While her chosen writing implement has matured, she still enjoys weaving stories that both entertain and make people think. She is one of the founders of FSF Publications. Kira currently lives in Arizona with her husband, Will.